TINDER & FLINT

By
Matthew Hinsley

Art by
Billy Garretsen

EnvisionArts

Austin

First EnvisionArts Hardcover Edition, February 2016

Cover Design by Billy Garretsen

Author Photo by David Tietz

Artist Photo by John Gibson

Published by EnvisionArts, LLC.

ISBN 978-1-365-23082-0

www.tinderandflintbooks.com

For Glenda

My deepest thanks go to fellow adventurers Joe Williams II, Quentin Lucas, Joseph Palmer, Travis Marcum, Amelia Devivo, and Glenda Lee, without whom this story could not exist. Thank you to my editors Jessica Hagemann, Glenda Lee, Rebecca Snedden, and Robert Knapp. I am so grateful for Billy Garretsen's talent, imagination, and enthusiasm for all things badass. To my dear readers who have encouraged *Tinder & Flint* from its inception: Thank you for beginning this journey with me—we're just getting started!

Contents

Since boyhood he'd been the strongest person he ever knew.

Chapter One
BOUDREAUX

Everything hurt. His insides were bruised and mushy from all the force trauma. The parts of his skin that he could feel were screaming from the dirty, clawed wounds that seemed to cover every inch of his exposed flesh.

It was so freezing down here that Boudreaux wasn't sure if the numbness in his elbows and forearms was from the cold or some bodily response to the many repeated blows of their studded clubs. Once they had overrun him, and his strength failed, he had doubled over and tried to protect his face. His arms had taken the lion's share of the beating at the end.

Chapter One

The piggy creatures had surprised him in his sleep. *There's a first time for everything*, he thought bitterly. Boudreaux was nearly impossible to surprise—he prided himself on it. He had slept in his armor. After the long travel day he had not been motivated to take it off before falling asleep. It was probably the only reason he'd survived.

If he'd come quietly, allowed the smelly, slimy bastards to bind him and drag him off to whatever torment they had planned, no doubt he would have avoided the damage and pain he had sustained during capture.

But Boudreaux didn't do *quiet* very well.

Since boyhood he'd been the strongest person he ever knew. When suddenly awoken the night before, he had felt their carefully threaded rope tightening around his ankles and then smelled the foul huddled shapes all around him. One of them loomed directly above his head, holding a cruel blade just inches from his right eye.

Boudreaux exploded. This was just the kind of thing he was built for. In seconds he'd grabbed the blade-hand of his nearest assailant and, breaking its arm backwards, he had buried its weapon deep in its own ribs. In the course of the violent movement, his legs had shredded the loose binding, and he'd found himself on his feet surrounded by ripples of dark movement. The startled shriek of his first kill gurgled quickly to silence.

But not before they all knew.

It's hard to say how many he'd overcome. He never made it to his weapons. If he had been armed, the night would have ended differently indeed. Instead he crushed them together, hurled them at one another and into trees, and tore them apart with his bare hands for as long as he possibly could, for hours it seemed, but then again battle time is slower than meal time.

There were simply too many. Boudreaux knew he had lost a lot of blood, but not before he and the earth all around him were glistening and slippery with theirs. Eventually they'd worn him down, and at some sad point in the final clubbing, his mind quit and the world went totally black.

Live. I have to live.

The beasts were returning. They made far more noise down here than they did outside sneaking around his camp, so Boudreaux heard them approach well before they arrived. A sharp intake of breath behind him, and a stifled whimper near his right side, told him he was not the only prisoner abducted in the night.

His eyes were swollen and thoroughly crusted closed with dried blood. They opened with effort, though, and fighting nausea, he looked around the dank space. It was near black, but one of the many gifts from his elf mother was excellent eyesight in the dark. Two children, a boy and a girl, though bound at the wrists and ankles, had somehow slithered together for warmth and comfort overnight. Behind him an older man in torn clothing and manacles seemed delirious.

Boudreaux, too, was bound in some crude iron restraints. He had little doubt that at full strength, and given some time, he could break free of them. The thought actually made him smile inside a bit.

They have no idea.

Chapter One

Moments later, torchlight flooded the small cell. The door banged open and a stench of rank breath and sweaty malodor accompanied two phenomenally ugly creatures. Black beady eyes were set deep atop large and misshapen piggy snouts with teeth protruding in all directions. A steady stream of snot and slobber glistened and ran from nostrils and mouths that seemed unable to completely control their contents.

They were about four feet tall and their twisted, compact bodies belied the coiled strength of beings that had probably fought each other for survival from the day they were born. Their red and black blotchy hides bore wisps of long, matted grey hair that did not cover the scars of years living their violent ways.

Boudreaux yelled. He didn't mean to. It was unintelligible anyway, some mix of "no," "stop," and "don't." His plan had been to remain quiet and compliant and to attract as little attention as possible, at least for the time being.

So much for that.

But the pig thing had just grabbed that little girl so roughly. He yanked her from the ground and clear into the air by the binding on her wrists. Boudreaux knew that, at the very least, something in her shoulder had torn. Yet it was Boudreaux who had screamed. The girl remained totally silent, and after being deposited on her feet, she just stood there, staring straight ahead, swaying.

The second pig man came shambling toward Boudreaux's shout. Its filthy boot struck Boudreaux in the face, causing him to bleed afresh. A string of guttural admonishments and spittle flowed from its crooked mouth, followed by labored wheezes that might have been laughter.

The boy was standing now, and so was the older man behind him. It was clear they were going somewhere and as soon as it seemed he wouldn't be struck again for moving, Boudreaux stood as well. He was careful to make standing seem more difficult than it really was.

There were more of them outside the cell. One entered with a long chain and snaked it through the manacles of all the prisoners.

Time to move.

A massive and terrifying stone effigy lorded over the hall.

Chapter Two
CAVERNS

The place was a subterranean maze. Large natural caverns, connected by tunnels that looked as though they had been dug out by thousands of claws, had paths beaten into existence by the ceaseless scuffling of feet in boots of leather and iron.

The prisoners started out slowly. The children moved with surprisingly sure and resolute steps. Sandwiched between them and the older man, who seemed not always to understand which direction the procession was headed, Boudreaux feigned weakness just enough to slow the march and conceal the man's feeble constitution. In his experience with both slavers and eaters—he'd had dealings with more of both than he cared to recall—he knew that any prisoner marked as too weak to walk or work would not be long for this world.

Chapter Two

I'll keep these people safe.

The pace quickened, however. While a brisk clip helped direct the old man behind him, once the pig men began dragging them faster, the kids had difficulty keeping up. The boy, second in line, stubbed his toe and fell. But the procession did not stop. The pigs just pulled harder and faster. The kid was dragged by his wrists between Boudreaux and the girl until he could regain his footing.

They passed through several large chambers. *God, there are a lot of them.* The creatures in each worked noisily with dirt or wood or metal. When the prisoners came in, they stopped and stared or sneered or yelled in their vile language. Boudreaux took several hard objects to his face and torso, then realized they were cracked bones hurled by a gleeful onlooker.

Celebrate, you bastards. Soon I'll know every twist and turn of this dark hole. I'll know where to find you.

And then he saw it.

Boudreaux would never forget what came next. He did not know, of course, that it would change his life forever. He didn't actually have any idea what it was, but he knew it was bad.

The right side of the tunnel split open to reveal a huge, brilliantly-lit marble hall. Surely his captors had tunneled into it by accident, for in Boudreaux's experience, only dwarves built with the magnificent precision, and beauty, and attention to detail apparent here.

But there were no dwarves. Rather, a massive and terrifying stone effigy lorded over the hall, leering with a hateful intensity. Inanimate though it was, its gaze froze the prisoners in their tracks and rendered them heedless of their captor's hauling chain.

Unable to move forward, they stared aghast at the demon statue's black saber teeth, and the enormous horned wings that swept bat-like from powerful shoulders. But the eyes were the worst. A collective shudder rippled down the line.

The evil monstrosity towered over something strange that Boudreaux would turn over and over in his mind, long after the pigs finally hauled them past the marble hall, and on further into the dark tunnel.

There appeared to be an opening, huge and irregularly shaped, into some other place entirely. It hung like a broken window splattered and yawning. Through it, Boudreaux glimpsed winged lizards silhouetted against a red sky. Another team of pig things, at the orders of a large man in black robes, prodded a chain of ten morose prisoners, too similar to Boudreaux's own sorry party, into the gaping rift.

Hell, Boudreaux thought. *I think I've just looked straight into Hell.*

She produced six large blossoms and held them out proudly.

Chapter Three
THE ROAD

"Hang on, guys!" X'andria yelled as she bounded from the road. Again.

Ohlen fixed a practiced and patient grin on his face but couldn't keep his hands from sliding to rest on his hips. Gnome stopped adroitly, his featherlight steps halting as though instantly and magically glued to the earth.

Unfortunately Arden's gaze and attention were fully devoted to a strange bird flying high above them in the blue cloudless sky. Not only did he fail to stop, he plowed at a brisk clip directly into Gnome.

Chapter Three

At just over three feet tall, Gnome was accustomed to strangers not always registering his presence. In truth, much of the time he preferred it that way, since as the company scout, reconnaissance expert, and occasional thief, he often specifically sought to go unnoticed. But Gnome had a huge temper for a small person, and ever since entering the world of big people, being stepped on, knocked over, or squashed were all high on his list of least-favorite things. Arden, in this case, managed to do them all in the span of about three seconds.

Thankfully, when Gnome was truly furious, he tended to revert to his native tongue for his expletive outbursts, and none in the party but X'andria could understand the language of the little people. She was too far away to hear.

"Anything good?" Ruprecht shouted to X'andria, as soon as he was able to control his laughter.

It was a perfect day. The road had been clear since they set out that morning. Not a soul in sight. The sun was shining, the breeze was gentle, and they were heading to Westover. Arden had actually been born in Westover, though his family left when he was just a boy. No one else in the party had ever visited. Since providing safe passage for a wealthy trader and his entourage from the coast to Bridgeton, the friends were briefly out of work. The trader would be returning to the coast in a week or so, and no doubt he'd require their services again, but that left just enough time for them to visit Arden's birthplace and for him to pay respects to his ancestors.

"Oooooh, they're beautiful!" trilled X'andria, her shock of dark red hair bobbed out of sight over the edge of the berm.

"What did you find?" Ruprecht called, earth-brown robes waving as he turned toward her voice.

"Gnome, listen man, I'm so sorry," Arden was dusty and still seated on the ground. "I was tracking this bird I've never seen before and I just wasn't paying attention. I am *so* sorry."

"I don't wanna hear it, big man," growled Gnome, standing and swatting dust from his sleek black leathers. "Just keep your big stupid thoughts behind that clumsy face of yours. And are you sitting, talking to me so that we'll be the same height?" Arden made a face in recognition of the direction this was going but couldn't articulate a protest fast enough. Gnome shouted now, "Because if you are, **and I now see that in fact you are**, you have no idea how rude that is!"

Gnome was still rolling out the admonishment when Ohlen, in flowing white, appeared beside them as though borne over by the breeze. His rich baritone soothed, "Gnome and Arden, I implore you both to take a moment and reflect on each other's path and position."

And then he did the thing.

On one knee, Ohlen placed his left hand on Arden's right shoulder, and his right hand on Gnome's left shoulder. And that was it. The air cleared between them, Arden's guilt melted away with Gnome's indignation in a wave of understanding and empathy that left them lighter than they had been even before the whole episode.

"Huge score!" cried X'andria, skipping back to the road. "Rotweed!" Tearing huge smelly leaves into little squares and stuffing them into a fold in her night-blue robes, she continued "And look at these, Ruprecht, I found *Crocus blossoms*!" She produced six large blossoms and held them out proudly.

The scowl was creeping slowly back onto Gnome's face when, just in time, X'andria prattled on, "And you'll love these, Gnome, I could hardly believe it when I spotted them," with a flourish, "*grasshoppers*!"

"I don't know how you do it, X'an," Gnome allowed. "I've been looking for these little buggers for months. I was starting to think I'd never see another one." Lightning fast, Gnome plucked the live grasshoppers from X'andria's carefully cupped hands, and they disappeared into his black tunic.

The friends walked on. Arden resumed intently looking skyward, but everyone agreed he should take the lead just in case any more abrupt stops befell their march. Usually rather quiet, Ohlen found himself engaged with Gnome in a lengthy discussion concerning the character of the merchant who had hired them.

Ohlen was privately disappointed with the trader's comportment, especially his tendency to take young wives almost as frequently, it seemed, as he traveled to and from Bridgeton. But he felt obligated to challenge Gnome's brash suggestion that, on the return trip to the coast, they should strip the fat devious man of all his clothes and belongings, leave him naked on the side of the road, and invite his wives to abandon him and join them, instead, on their next adventure.

Gnome was joking, to be sure, but Ohlen didn't really do joking.

This left Ruprecht and X'andria trudging along at the rear of the group, engrossed in stories of fantastic and impossibly potent magical energy, trading tales of artifacts whispered of in guild halls, and dreaming aloud about harnessing the mysterious invisible energy of the universe with words and runes and deeds and dust. All the while, X'andria's bright eyes darted and scanned for useful items at the roadside, or just glimpses of beauty that struck her fancy.

Ohlen and Arden were the first to notice something was wrong. For Ohlen, he felt a sorrowful disruption creep into the atmosphere on a dark ethereal wave. The blood around his stomach ran cold, and his core became tense and prickly.

Arden's nose alerted him first, and caused him to tear his eyes abruptly away from the sky while reaching instinctively for the hilt of his sword. It was the distant smell of smoke and fire mixed with death.

Death comes in many forms, and all of them have smells.

"Weapons," hissed Gnome.

*Normally neat and well-tended buildings lay in toppled heaps of rubble
and thatch, the town's quaint beauty reduced to blackened hulls.*

Chapter Four
WESTOVER

Training, talent and instinct are an amazingly powerful cocktail when mixed together in pure form and ample measure.

In moments, and in wordless harmony, they left the road and hugged the shallow bank. X'andria and Ruprecht lacked the super senses of Ohlen and Arden, and they did not have Gnome's speed and ultra-perception, but they knew their friends, trusted them implicitly, and dashed to the roadside seconds behind their forward compatriots.

And there they lay breathing, listening, sensing.

Chapter Four

Ohlen broke the silence first.

"Something has gone terribly wrong in Westover. But I do not believe we are in imminent danger. People have suffered greatly, there is evil at work, but no wicked forces come this way. Arden, do you concur?"

"The earth and air have stopped talking," breathed Arden, sampling the air with a series of rapid sniffs. "Small animals are gone. I just now caught fire and death on the wind. Perhaps three miles away. No struggle or heavy travel on this road, however. So I agree: whatever plagues Westover isn't coming to or from this direction."

The dozen silver-tipped darts X'andria had purchased in Bridgeton were heavy, cruel and beautiful things. The long barbed tips were designed to cause maximum damage on both entrance and exit. Eagle-feather flights extended from heavy polished oak shafts shaped like teardrops that felt fabulous in the hand, and added considerable weight and power to the flight. X'andria was a crack shot, and the moment she saw the darts she knew she had to have them. She rolled one nervously in her right hand as she fell into mute step behind Gnome.

Arden was in front. He preferred it that way, and so did everyone else. His skill at scouting and tracking made him the company's ideal eyes and ears and he was, frankly, one tough sonofabitch. If he had to choose, he'd fight left-handed, and his left hand rested now on the hilt of a sword that had been his father's, and his father's father's before that. But he was almost equally lethal with his right hand, and lately he'd taken to training with a newer, shorter sword on the right, while wielding the family weapon on the left.

Arden's large leather field satchel hung on his back, the strap slung diagonally across his chest. Heavy with armor and gear, each step he took caused smaller pouches to swing around him like baubles adorning a jester's hat.

The band stayed off the road, doing their best to go silently and unnoticed. As they walked on, there sprang up stretches of wooded areas and they hugged the tree line whenever possible. From time to time Arden held up a hand and they all froze until he was satisfied they were not walking into a threat.

Always stoic, Ohlen glided along cloudlike in deep concentration. It was not often clear that his eyes were even open, as if he navigated the physical world just by sensing good and evil, order and chaos, energy and void.

So his friends were not surprised when, even in the absence of any visual indication, Ohlen breathed softly, "We're here."

They couldn't see Westover, but Ohlen could feel the deflated energy of the town on the other side of the grove of trees they had been skirting. Once focused on it, however, Arden could see signs through the trees as well, and after brief discussion it was decided they would approach the town through the forest.

It was late afternoon. Gnome's thoughts turned practical. No matter what they found, they would have to establish camp within the hour to utilize what daylight remained to set up the appropriate defensive measures. Danger was clearly present, which meant no fires, no hot meals, and staggered overnight shifts, sleeping dressed and armed.

What were routine maneuvers for Arden and Ohlen over brambles, questionable ivy, and fallen logs, were obstacles for Gnome, yet through the trees he was the fastest and, by far, the quietest of them all. All the while his lamp-like eyes scanned for ideal places to establish camp, trees to look out from, routes to escape through, saplings to bend, arm, and bind into trip traps. As they neared the town, he identified the perfect spot to make camp and marked it in his memory.

The scene before them was horrifying.

Westover was a still-smoldering ruin. Normally neat and well-tended buildings lay in toppled heaps of rubble and thatch, the town's quaint beauty reduced to blackened hulls.

Ohlen didn't need to see the bodies for his guts to twist inside him. The way he was wired, he had begun feeling the agony of their tortured deaths before he had even entered the wood. Ruprecht felt bile rise in his throat and looked toward the heavens in an effort to steady himself. X'andria just stared open-mouthed at each still corpse in turn, her horror an overwhelming sadness.

Anger. Anger defined both Arden and Gnome. Gnome was prone to rage anyhow, and brutal injustice, for Gnome, meant visiting swift vengeance upon those responsible.

Arden's family had taken him away before he was old enough to really remember Westover. But these were his people. Through the dirt, blood, soot, and disfigurement, he saw dozens of faces that could easily have been his brothers and sisters, his mom and dad, his children—blond hair matted haphazardly in dispirited clumps.

His father's sword appeared in his left hand and he stormed forward looking for something or someone to destroy, someone to make pay for the atrocity. He raced noisily through the streets, forest-green cape flapping behind him, each new victim fresh fuel for his fury. He searched in vain for those responsible.

Nothing lived. Whoever had done this was long gone. It was obvious, really. But there was no talking to Arden in this state.

"We must bury the dead," sighed Ohlen heavily.

"Yes," agreed Ruprecht, "and you and I will bless them, each and every one. While they lost their lives to tragedy and pain in this world, they will float in ethereal love and kindness in the next." He looked solemnly into Ohlen's bottomless slate-grey eyes.

"X'an, let's make camp," the glowering Gnome stalked back toward the forest with X'andria at his side. "Fifty paces in, forty paces north," he called over his shoulder without looking back. "Shout if you need us, we'll make up basics and be out to help carry in half an hour."

It did not take long for Ohlen and Ruprecht to find the cemetery. On the north side of the village was a neat little gated plot with many small graves and, thankfully, a mausoleum. Feeling slightly guilty, they forced the door of the mausoleum and walked inside.

Darkness. Darkness and damp, musty earth.

Ruprecht felt inside one of the countless tiny pockets in his simple brown robes for coal dust. With a pinch in his fingers, and holy mutterings on his breath, he froze and called forth for light.

The weight of his deity, no matter what he asked, was always phenomenal. It lasted for just a split second, but for that one instant he felt like he stood at the bottom of an ocean, gasping for breath beneath inconceivable weight, yet reaching for the beauty shimmering high above.

Brilliant light, brighter even than the waning afternoon, flooded the dark mausoleum. Rats scurried in all directions, vacating an otherwise clean room. To the right, stone stairs descended into what was surely the crypt.

"We will bury the dead here, in their ancestors' resting place," intoned Ohlen somberly. They left the still-shining mausoleum to gather bodies, Ruprecht's heart still pounding in his ears.

21

Chapter Four

Arden had found someone. Several streets away, Ohlen and Ruprecht could hear him yelling. They ran. She cowered on the ground and Arden brandished his sword above her, gesticulating, and shouting—the coil of rope he wore at his waist had nearly worked itself loose in the agitation. Arden wanted to know *who she was, what had happened, why had she lived, was she* **responsible**?

Instinctively Ruprecht hastened to Arden and, with gentle whispered coaxing, led him away and even managed to get him to lower his weapon. Arden's protests and rapid breaths gave way to barely stifled sobs, before his knees trembled and he broke down completely in heaving hysterics, sinking into Ruprecht's arms.

Like a white dove landing on broken earth, Ohlen knelt fluidly by the Westoveran woman and laid his hand on her forearm. He said nothing, but peacefulness radiated powerfully from his compassionate countenance. She hesitantly turned her tear-streaked face to meet his glowing kindness.

After a short, hushed discussion, Arden consented to carry, and Ohlen set about blessing and burying the dead. Ruprecht gingerly led the traumatized woman, Rowena, to find Gnome's camp. The camp was, of course, right where Gnome had said it would be.

"Stop!" Gnome shouted. Ruprecht and Rowena stopped. "See those two broad leaves by your right foot? Don't step on those or you'll regret it." Eyes narrowing suspiciously, Gnome then growled, "Who's that with you, Ruprecht?"

Ruprecht made introductions. Tears filled X'andria's enormous green eyes as she grasped the rattled Westoveran woman's soiled hands in sympathy, but after several quiet moments she and Gnome left to assist with the burial; Ruprecht stayed at camp to tend to Rowena.

Of all the requests he could make of his god, healing was the holiest. Ruprecht had never asked for more than one miracle in the same day. He knew he would be totally exhausted. Rowena consented to lie down while he placed one hand on her forehead and the other on her stomach. He chanted, he connected, he thanked for the light, he asked for health, he writhed under the weight of his god's greatness once more. It was such brilliance he thought he would never see darkness again, so much pressure he felt as though his pounding ears and his pulsing eyes would hemorrhage inside his skull.

And then nothing. The world went black for Ruprecht.

Hours later, when he awoke, Ruprecht's friends had returned. Rowena was seated nearby, silent and grieving, but somewhat restored. Westover had been cleared of its corpses, Gnome's traps were set, the night watch schedule had been agreed upon, and the simple dried meals were passed around. Arden packed and held his wooden pipe, but contented himself with smelling its aroma, after Gnome's terse warning about fire and smoke.

It was time to hear Rowena's tale.

"Don't let Young Olssen's pig man get you tonight."

Chapter Five
ROWENA'S TALE

The creatures come only at night.

At first the villagers reported seeing strange animals in the fields and forests. There were all kinds of speculation that they were wolves or wild boars. I remember the night that the Olssen boy came panting into West's Inn with wild eyes and an even wilder tale of a huge, man-sized boar in the woods that stood on its hind legs, looked him in the eye, and raised a fist as if to strike him.

Young Olssen went on and on about the eyes and the teeth, and the more he went on, the funnier it seemed to all of us. Two days later his story was all over town, and I heard people saying goodnight with a chuckle, telling each other, "Don't let Young Olssen's pig man get you tonight."

Rowena shivered beneath a thin wool blanket of Arden's, and

tears welled in her eyes.

Young Olssen was the first to go missing. He was so tired of people making fun of him, and not believing his story, that he set out a few nights later to prove us all wrong. He headed west into the forest with his little dagger in his hand, and elder Olssen's helmet on his head. His dad told him not to go, that it was silly to try to prove everyone wrong, that some day he'd grow up and understand. I'll never forget the tremble in that poor boy's voice, from being so mad at us, and, I'm sure, from being scared of what he might find, when he yelled back, "I'll show you, you'll see," as he stormed off into the night.

Well, he never got the chance to show us. I doubt he ever showed anything to anyone after that night. But we certainly did come to see. Townsfolk began disappearing almost nightly after that. We had emergency meetings, set up night patrols, and added strict curfews so that no one but the patrolmen were to roam after dark.

Our safety measures were effective. But I'm afraid they were a bit too effective. For a week or so, no one was lost, and everyone was thinking the worst might be over. But then those things started coming into the village and plucking entire families right out of their homes as they slept.

One night they encountered a patrol and they slaughtered each and every member of the squad, including elder Olssen. Everyone heard that fight, and the bawling and screaming. Terrible sounds.

*When we ventured from our homes the next morning, two of those vile fiends were lying dead on the ground. They are like nothing anyone has ever seen. I can see why young Olssen described what he saw that night as a boar on its hind legs. Their smushed-in faces have snouts more than noses, and their mouths sprout teeth that stick out in nearly every direction. Their hands though—*and here Rowena swallowed hard—*their hands are human.*

Rowena shook violently and was unable to speak for some time. Had there been tears left in her, no doubt they would have flowed. Eventually she continued.

They wear things just like we do. They have armor and boots and one had a club with spikes. The other had rope coiled around it. What could they be? They are like horrible animal people! Like hell belched them up to torment us and drag us back down with them into the fire.

And at the word "fire" there was a whoosh, a thud, and a strangled cry in the night. One of Gnome's trip traps had found a target, and what followed was chaos.

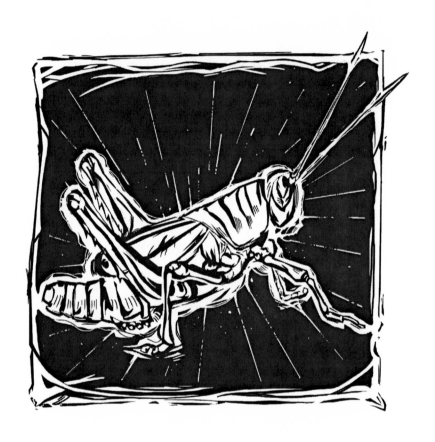

His dexterous fingers fished a grasshopper from one of the many pockets inside his tunic and, holding it aloft, he remembered his lessons and imagined light.

Chapter Six
THE NIGHT

Although Gnome had successfully persuaded everyone that a fire would invite danger, danger, it seemed, had shown up uninvited.

The forest sprang to life around them. Whoever the intruders were, they had managed to get close, in large numbers, without being detected.

Another of Gnome's traps found purchase. X'andria spun and squinted into the blackness. She had extraordinary eyesight in the dark, and her palms itched to throw her deadly darts.

She saw two, very close. X'andria could not tell what they were, but she could see that they had heads, and heads meant eyes, and eyes meant a spot between which any beast could be killed. In six seconds both creatures lay twitching, dying on the ground. Her first kill shot cut down the right hand assailant before it hit the edge of the small clearing that was their camp. The second, however, seeing her attack and hearing the morbid surprise of its companion, rushed forward. Only then did X'andria get her first dark glimpse of the hellish fiends.

Gnome summoned his own powers of concentration. Focus was hard to maintain in the midst of being attacked by unseen creatures near a brutally decimated village of innocents, but Gnome was rock solid where others panicked. His dexterous fingers fished a grasshopper from one of the many pockets inside his tunic and, holding it aloft, he remembered his lessons and imagined light. Not just any light, though, he imagined balls of light surrounding them in a twenty-foot radius, spaced evenly apart, and located both on the ground and in the trees. Gnome imagined lighting the forest to reveal their assailants, but not themselves. And with that crystal image shining in his mind, with intent held firmly by his will, a power word tore from his lips. *Mjargi'lig.* Light.

Uttering the word caused Gnome to feel like pieces of his chest, throat, and brain were exiting through his mouth. The grasshopper, held aloft, separated and morphed into brilliant colored balls of light and moved majestically, as directed, into the precise formation Gnome had envisioned. For Gnome, the illumination seemed to take one agonizing minute to complete. He pitched forward to the earth gasping, but his face was agleam in a rare smile.

The glow of Gnome's spell revealed twenty creeping beasts. Fear and surprise registered on their piggy faces, especially when they saw their fallen comrades.

It was Arden's cue to act. This was the fight he had been steeling himself for since their nightmarish arrival in Westover earlier that day. He rushed forward with a berserk cry, swords springing to both hands as if out of thin air, and cut his way into the thickest crush of the beasts. He cleaved as he ran. His pace did not even slow as both weapons danced and arced, trailing crimson drops in their wake.

Ruprecht and Ohlen protectively encircled Rowena, who was hugging her knees on the ground. One of the monsters crept near. Clutching a rusty small two-headed axe, its feeble mind fixated on the still targets.

These three will bleed.

It felt like his left shoulder and arm had been dipped in icy water—Ohlen knew this feeling, the feeling of evil. He had always been a super sensate. It was something that made his boyhood difficult, actually, until the brotherhood taught him to control and amplify it. In his later training, they would place him in deep stone dungeons with slimy walls, hundreds of rats, and the omnipresence of urine and feces. But none of those things bothered Ohlen. He was there to experience evil. His task was to determine who, of the inmates, possessed the purest evil of all. The games were easy for him, really, and he was never wrong. He was often surprised, however, that the jailors were no less evil than many of their wards.

Ohlen turned to face their attacker, its axe aloft, its intent telegraphed clearly through the ether. He accessed the warmth within him. Finding the powerful golden sphere beneath his solar plexus, Ohlen pushed into the icy black cold in his shoulder and arm and felt the evil creeping inside him immolate like dry parchment in a raging hearth.

The beast's face lost all determination and its axe clattered to the ground. It turned and ran. Had there been anyone looking on, it would have appeared as though the slim white-robed Ohlen had dispatched it simply by upturning his palms.

Gnome intercepted the fleeing monster—a shadow falling from its perch in a tree above—and drove his dagger down through the top of its skull.

In all, twenty-two beasts were killed. X'andria felled four more in as many shots, and Gnome dispatched three, beyond the brutal and efficient work of his two trip traps. The remains of all the others were being slowly and deliberately cleaned from Arden's glistening weapons. X'andria walked among the dead to retrieve, sanitize, and store her precious darts.

They awoke in the morning having had no more unwanted visitors in the night.

"Goblins," announced Arden with conviction. "I've only seen skulls before at the guild, and drawings, and these are them," he gestured disdainfully at the limp pile of bodies several yards away. "They kill any living thing they encounter, eat their prey and each other, and inhabit the dwellings of those they destroy rather than build their own."

Ignoring Ohlen's disapproving looks and harrumphs, Gnome and X'andria scoured the pile of rapidly souring carcasses for valuables. They were disappointed not to find much, but what little trinkets and coins of value they came across were stowed in their leather backpacks.

"There is a man," muttered Rowena to no one in particular, nibbling a dry biscuit, "who lives in the forest on the other side of Westover."

She stared glumly at the ground.

X'andria shivered and looked around at the huge trees...

Chapter Seven
THE MAN IN THE FOREST

According to Rowena, the man was a hermit. Though rarely seen, he was reputed to possess great power and a friendly disposition: two traits that did not always come packaged together. She felt if anyone would be able to help, it would be him. She had never been to his remote cottage in the woods, but she knew it lay in the same general direction as the place young Olssen had first laid eyes on the pig men.

"Wait a minute," Gnome cut in, "no one is actually considering going west to find this mystery man, are they? West is where these *things* were first seen, it's clearly where they're coming from, and so I'm trying to figure out why we haven't already started heading back east to Bridgeton?"

Silence.

"Seriously?" Gnome was getting irritated, "we can get a *job* bringing Fatso from Bridgeton back to the coast! He will *pay* us to do something way easier than walk west into that forest." Pointing and getting more animated, "I realize we all had a *ball* risking our lives last night in the death dance with those..."

"Goblins," offered Arden sullenly, eyes on the ground.

"Goblins," Gnome continued. "But those things don't even carry anything valuable. Ask X'andria! And nothing we do, no number of butchered goblins, will bring back Westover."

More silence.

"That may not be technically true," Ohlen broke in. "I blessed and buried many Westoverans yesterday afternoon. More than I care to recall. But not nearly as many, I venture, as must have lived in this town before the massacre. That leads me to only one conclusion: that innocent people were taken and may yet be very much alive."

"**Injustice!**" Ruprecht's eyes were tightly closed and his voice emanated as though coming from the air all around them. "What happened here is a wrong that must be righted. It is an act of malice that will grow unless cut down. I am compelled to go westward." They were all staring at him open-mouthed when Ruprecht's kind eyes popped back open with a slight shake of his head, and his familiar benevolent smile returned beneath his thick brown beard.

Arden took to his feet. At the realization that innocents might be in peril of enslavement, torment, or death by goblin, even Gnome eventually agreed their group was honor-bound to find and free any would-be prisoners, and quickly.

Over her feeble but persistent protests, it was decided Rowena would walk to Bridgeton to report everything she knew to anyone who would listen. She would leave immediately so as to move in daylight, with a day's worth of food, and with Ruprecht's blessing.

Rowena knelt and Ruprecht placed his hands on her shoulders.

She was amazed at how warm they felt. She could tell he was saying something, muttering continuously. His hands became so hot they were almost painful, yet at the same time they radiated a life-giving energy throughout her entire being. His body tensed, and for a moment it felt almost like he was lifted slightly from the earth. And then it was done.

Rowena felt powerful. Invincible. At once acutely aware of Westover's recent tragedies, of the irrevocable loss of her friends and family, Rowena was also buoyed by a strong sense of love and gratitude. She said her goodbyes and stepped confidently into the morning.

It was time for the rest of the group to move out as well.

The path west into the forest began wide and bright, but after only thirty minutes of brisk walking, the trees closed in. Mountains loomed in the distance. Arden slowed their pace from time to time to study the myriad tracks crisscrossing the path.

"What are you finding, Arden?" inquired X'andria.

"There's not been a lot of traffic here since the last rain. Mostly animals. I think I'm getting pretty good at spotting goblins. They all seem to wear the same boots we saw on the ones in Westover. A bit smaller than most men. But I'm rarely seeing them on the path, and when I do, they are not going along it at all, they're cutting across out of the forest on one side and directly back into it on the other. They must prefer to travel under cover."

X'andria shivered and looked around at the huge trees—the fingers of her left hand felt their way nervously toward the jade necklace around her neck, her one piece of jewelry. It was probably her imagination, but it sure seemed that at Arden's words the air cooled and the light dimmed.

They resumed walking westward. Rowena had said the hermit lived half way to the mountains, and in another hour that's approximately where the group found themselves. Ohlen, gliding along, stopped and placed the index and middle fingers of his right hand against the short white hair frosting his right temple and inclined his head forward slightly.

"I am unsure what it is, but I can say with certainty that *there* lies a force unlike anything else in this forest." Like a compass needle, Ohlen's arm pointed north into the trees.

"Three hours, people," announced Gnome, all business. "Light will be gone in four and we must have the camp prepared for a worst-case scenario ambush before then."

"Getting there will not take long, Gnome," Ohlen replied. "We are close."

Gone were the small woods of Westover. Here huge trees choked a complex environment of thick green vegetation and orange moss, damp soil and rotting logs. The group's march was slow going. Arden cut through underbrush with his small sword and scanned for signs of anything he could identify. Uncharacteristically, Gnome's lungs began to wheeze from leaping up and down over huge fallen limbs.

Ruprecht gasped suddenly and toppled over clutching his right ankle.

"Damn," he said, "what the hell was that?"

A helmet—banded iron. Stepping over a particularly large log, Ruprecht had not seen it lying upside down in the soft earth.

Everyone stared. Gashed and dented, the helmet had seen

violence. Ruprecht, splayed on the ground, picked it up but immediately dropped it. The helmet's lining was caked with congealed blood and patches of white blond hair.

Upon trying to stand, Ruprecht realized he could not walk. His ankle injury merely compounded the weakness he still felt from blessing Rowena, not to mention the extreme spiritual exertion of the day before.

X'andria began to worry. Maybe this whole thing wasn't such a good idea after all. She eyed Ruprecht, downed and lame. Her gaze then slid over to Gnome, who masked his doubt under a hardened veneer of tough resolve. Gnome, too, was peering back at Ruprecht, lips parted slightly in consternation, sweat dripping from the tip of his nose.

Gnome.

X'andria first saw Gnome's eyes.

She had nicked a small satin purse held carelessly by a clean boy bouncing dandily along the street with his parents. They had yelled, and she had run, and now she was back at the low-ceilinged hovel she and the other orphan children inhabited.

A single candle burned on a wooden stool they used as a table. Each night when "Mama and Papa," as they called themselves, came stooping into the dingy space with dinner, the children placed whatever they had pilfered that day on the stool before eating. The purse was empty, but the satin was fine, and it would be enough.

This night, upon her return, X'andria's quick eyes immediately registered two suspended orbs in the far corner brightly reflecting back the light of the single flickering candle. Too big to be eyes, she turned to approach the glowing mysteries. But by the time she made it to the corner, they had vanished.

The morning's light brought X'andria's first full view of Gnome. At a glance he appeared to be just another child—but he wasn't. He had dark features, a defined jaw, and positively enormous round eyes. He seemed older than the others, yet he was their size. And, like X'andria, his ears vanished in points extending up into his frazzled mop of thick dark hair. He was not an elf, but he was not human either, and X'andria's longing for kinship poked urgently at her consciousness.

Gnome rarely spoke in the early days. His language was rough, and communication was difficult, and he seemed to trust no one. But X'andria was persistent with her smiles and greetings, even in the absence of reciprocity, and ever-so-slowly he began to choose places nearer to her at meal times.

Gnome was a gifted thief. Nightly, where others produced meager trinkets and castaways, Gnome always delivered multiple gleaming metallic items. Coming up empty-handed meant no dinner at best, and punishment at worst. Their friendship truly began the night Gnome snuck a coin into X'andria's sweaty palm after the loaf of bread she'd stolen came up missing—likely devoured by some of the other unscrupulous urchins they lived with. X'andria would never forget Gnome's hint of a grin when she turned to see who was her benefactor.

They began roving together. X'andria was especially good at spotting marks, Gnome had near flawless execution. Between them they secretly stashed items away from the others, away from Mama and Papa. With the passing months X'andria, whose talent for language and memorization was unparalleled, taught Gnome to speak the language of humans more fluently.

They were out together on a bright warm day when X'andria saw something that stopped her in her tracks. A book in Elfish runes. It was clasped in the spotty gnarled hand of a stooped old man with a bald head and long white beard. He sat silently reading and sunning himself on a flat rock.

Gnome had superior instincts and registered the stutter in X'andria's steps instantly. They retreated behind a nearby tree. "The book!" she whispered urgently, her wide green eyes imploring.

Moments later they sauntered casually back around the wide trunk and walked in the direction of the old man on the rock. In a flash, Gnome snatched the book from its unsuspecting reader, and the two friends dashed away. X'andria's mind raced with excitement as she imagined reading Elfish once more.

But the excitement ran cold when both she and Gnome froze inexplicably in mid-air.

They could not speak, they could not turn to look at one another, they were suspended within their bodies as though time itself had stopped.

The old man shuffled noisily into view. He squinted down at the two of them and plucked his book back out of Gnome's still hand. He then regarded them in silence for several long moments.

"There's magic in you two," The Alchemist said quizzically. And their lives changed drastically after that.

Sensing Ruprecht's condition on the ground, Ohlen came to his side. Breathing deeply and bowing his head, Ohlen clasped Ruprecht's ankle in both hands, and Ruprecht experienced a sensation he'd never forget: like the pain was literally being squeezed out of him through the tips of his toes, pushed by a powerful fluid warmth.

Ohlen staggered to his feet. Whatever he had just done for Ruprecht had cost him dearly. X'andria and Gnome exchanged worried glances—they had never seen Ohlen display even the slightest sign of fatigue.

"Onward," ordered Ohlen, his rich voice betraying none of his weariness.

X'andria shook her head, trying to clear it of her doubt and of her childhood memories, and she and the others resumed their march.

"We're nearly there," panted Arden, "I'm seeing signs of cultivation, order, foot traffic." And the going indeed became easier with no more cutting through brambles and leaping over patches of mysterious moss, or stepping on the forlorn and abandoned helmets of eager boys.

The cottage door, when they arrived, gaped open. The gardens had, perhaps, once been well tended, but now grew wild and free. Gnome, silent and small, snuck swiftly inside like a burglar—the others followed cautiously.

Destruction. Everything that could be broken was broken. Even the built-in bookcase had been torn from its moorings, its contents strewn across the slatted wood floor.

Canvassing the room, Ruprecht found a vial of inky black liquid beneath the remains of the bed. X'andria, on her knees, closely examined what was left of the forgotten books for recognizable symbols. Gnome, on tiptoe, rifled through the splintered drawers looking for anything of value.

"Arden stop!" Ohlen boomed. The outdoorsman froze. None of them had ever heard Ohlen shout. "Step back."

Arden's outstretched hand curled around a fistful of air less than two inches away from a small black orb. He'd spotted it in a corner near the hearth. An innocuous children's toy. A marble.

"No one touch it," said Ohlen, calmer now, but clearly rattled. "What Arden has found is the disruption I sensed earlier on the path. Believe it or not, that small object seethes with the vilest hatred I have ever encountered... And that, my friends, is saying something."

Several things then happened at once.

As Ohlen carefully herded the accursed marble into an ornate round ivory case he carried on his person, an arrow whistled through the open door, entered X'andria's back, and sprouted through the front of her robes, disbelief and horror blooming in her great green eyes as they twitched to focus on its glistening point—and miles away beneath the earth, Boudreaux involuntarily roared.

With a primal roar, he stood completely upright, pulling the front of the cage up into a gaping maw with jagged metal teeth.

Chapter Eight
FREEDOM

I'm ready.

Boudreaux had been imprisoned for what must have been two days now. He, the old man, the boy, and the girl were locked in an iron cage with two other miserable inmates. Theirs was one of four such cages in the dungeon, and Boudreaux estimated there were just over twenty prisoners in all.

The pigs rarely entered the room, which was dark and unspeakably filthy. On what seemed like a completely random schedule, they would bang and stomp into the room heaving hideous cold slop through the bars that would land in piles on the floor and mix with god knows what that was already there.

Figuring the pig men's diet was almost exclusively meat, and that the garbage they threw at their prisoners was likely some scrappy derivative, Boudreaux came to the conclusion that ingesting as much of the runny material as possible would fuel his body's recovery. *Please let this not be human.* Scooping, chewing and swallowing was a matter of willpower. Keeping it down, however, was an epic battle of spirit and nerves, and one he frequently lost.

Even so, Boudreaux was recovering. His head was clear, his injuries were tolerable, and it was time to make a move.

The cages that held them were actually boxes of woven steel. Between his eyesight and the occasional torchlight at meal time, he knew the bottom of their cage was rusty from exposure to slop and excrement.

"I'll be back. Don't give up," he whispered to the girl. Of all the prisoners, she seemed the most in control of her wits. He moved to the front of the cage, bent his knees, and gripped the bottom of the grid. He then began to pull upward, pushing down onto the slimy rusty cage beneath with his powerful legs.

Breaking one of these pieces of iron would not have been difficult for Boudreaux. Woven fabric was another matter altogether. His preternatural strength caused an instant response, in that the mesh all around him began to bend and give as he strained against it. He stopped and restarted several times, noting that at each new attempt, the cage had slightly distended. In what would be his final push, he felt the first rigid rusted bar beneath his feet rupture and tear, then another, then another. With a primal roar, he stood completely upright, pulling the front of the cage up into a gaping maw with jagged metal teeth.

Unable to see, and too starved and drained to feel any more fear or hope, the other prisoners barely stirred at this unexpected outburst. Boudreaux stepped carefully out of the putrid cell. He had not meant to scream, and for several tense minutes he braced himself for the arrival of guards, but none came.

In darkness outside the cage he set about pushing it crudely back down and into a shape at least close to what it had been. *It's best if they stay here. It's disgusting, but where I'm going, and what I'm doing, will mean certain death for them.* "Hang in there," he breathed, before dashing to the door.

The tunnel was dimly lit by some light source flickering around a nearby corner. Plenty of light for Boudreaux, peering through the cracked door, to see that no one was in the immediate vicinity. He crept out and gently closed the door behind him.

The dungeon lay at the end of this particular passage. There was only one way to go. Boudreaux was elated. His entire plan rested on the prisoners being at the end of the network of tunnels. *Dungeons usually are the last stop*, he thought bitterly. This meant that as long as he annihilated absolutely everything in his forward path, nothing would reach the prisoners behind him. *Simple.*

Hugging the shadows, heart hammering like a drum, he crept to the bend in the tunnel. He stole a glance around the edge and quickly pulled his head back out of sight.

They smell me. He smiled his toothy broad grin for the first time in days. Drawing the pigs to himself around a corner was far better than advancing toward them, with no armor, in the open tunnel. In the latter scenario they could easily attack or, worse, run to alert the clan.

Two guards leaned sleepily on the long spears they used to prod captives through their cages. Upon noticing the odor of the dungeon wafting toward them, one guard reasoned that the door had come ajar, and went to perform its due diligence. Whatever thoughts crossed its small mind as they sauntered toward the bend, they most certainly did not include having its head violently twisted around backwards, or having the entire length of its spear thrust through its companion's heart, by a stark-naked and spectacularly muscular half-elf.

Six lethal seconds later Boudreaux froze to listen. His attack had been quiet, but the success of this whole endeavor rested on as much time as possible passing without the hoard realizing he was loose. He heard nothing, so he dragged his victims out of sight and stripped the larger one of his armor. The boots were hopeless. The chestplate was small but would do some good at least. A spear.

Thank heavens, a weapon.

Boudreaux's odds had just improved considerably.

He turned just in time to see oily jet black strands rushing and tumbling toward him, directly out of the fingertips of a tall, thin being in ominous black robes.

Chapter Nine
AT THE EDGE

X'andria's wide eyes fixed on the wet crimson point suspended in the air before her—blood dripped on her night-blue robes. Her head swam, indifferent to Gnome's anguished cries, Arden's blind fury, or Ruprecht's desperate hands dragging her from the line of fire.

At the moment Ohlen's ivory case clicked shut, sealing inside the mysterious black marble and its hideous energy, his senses returned to him. Ohlen had temporarily lost himself to the marble's dark power, and it had distracted him from premonition of the impending assault. With the marble neutralized, Ohlen comprehended the seriousness of X'andria's wound while realizing, with a shock, that they were completely surrounded. But there was something else, too, something darker and more powerful lying in wait.

Two goblins with small bows were stationed not fifteen feet from the door. They notched arrows as Arden stormed from the cottage, a blur of forest green and gleaming silver. One missed wide, the other hit him squarely in the right shoulder but failed to penetrate his heavy chain armor.

Arden sped across the short expanse heedless of the missile fire. His father's weapon danced in his left hand. Just before reaching the archers, he turned and planted his right foot bringing the hilt close in to his waist, the blade sticking out behind him. For increased power, and to cause maximum damage to the targets, he bent his knees low so that his entire body resembled a tight spring. Without breaking stride he exploded outward, driving the blade in a powerful upward arc clean through the torso of the nearest goblin and on past the arm and neck of the second. They slid sloppily into heaps on the ground.

Where are they all coming from?

A second arrow, from an unseen archer in the trees, caught Arden painfully in the right thigh, the head coming to rest against his femur. He rushed onward, ignoring the biting pain.

Ohlen was weak—he would need at least a day to replenish the outlay of energy from healing Ruprecht's ankle earlier that afternoon. Even so, he advanced into the waning daylight, his sword drawn.

They came quickly, like fish swimming around the liquid piles Arden had made of the archers. Ohlen could fight three of these beasts at a time, possibly four. But he would be facing far more this day, and if he survived at all, it would not be without injury. Just before engaging, however, Gnome materialized at his side, determination and venom glinting in his huge eyes.

Ohlen's spirit drank ravenously from the little man's certainty, like a parched traveler in the desert who has come upon a blessed oasis. As he raised his sword, so too did he project forth his most radiant self, cradling it with his mind and spirit as he and his little companion cut through the stupefied assailants all around them.

But that was it. Ohlen's reserve was spent. And the trees belched forth a fresh wave of slobbering fiends. As they clattered and scrambled their way toward Gnome and him, Ohlen caught sight of the Other: it was tall, shrouded in black robes, with long, deathly-white fingers extending slowly outward.

Arden found the hidden archer. It was behind a large tree hastily notching another arrow when he separated its head from its squat body. Liberating his blade from where it stuck in the tree trunk, Arden turned just in time to see oily jet black strands rushing and tumbling toward him—directly out of the fingertips of a tall, thin being in ominous black robes. The sticky fibrous ropes hit him with unexpected weight and pinned him awkwardly, right on top of the headless archer, to the large tree. He was hopelessly immobilized.

With a last sorrowful look at X'andria, Ruprecht grasped the leather-wrapped handle of his flail and raced to join Ohlen and Gnome against the advancing hoard. They came more slowly this time, calculating their approach, and Gnome took the opportunity to down two of the salivating wide-eyed leaders with weighted throwing daggers skillfully fired into their throats. Ruprecht settled into the left flank, Ohlen took the middle, Gnome the right.

The fight was grueling. While no goblin was a match for any of the three, many goblins meant nicks and cuts and fatigue. Many goblins meant arrows and axes flying from unexpected places, like the axe that buried itself deeply inside of Ohlen's left shoulder blade, drenching his white robes with an expansive blotch of deep liquid red.

They slipped in the bloody muck. They made mistakes. Gnome had slices all over his arms and a stinging gash on his face. Ruprecht's arms were so tired from the swinging and parrying and feinting that he knew he was reaching the end.

Many goblins lay dead or dying on the ground around them when, as though tied to an invisible leash, the standing combatants retreated slowly and warily backward to the tree line. There was much drooling and gnashing of teeth, cat calling and guttural jeering. Behind them came still more foul beasts. Finally, gliding into view, came the tall shrouded figure, face completely obscured in deep, dark folds.

Arden, invisible now save for his boots and a patch of light blond hair, struggled to the point of bleeding against his merciless animated bonds. He could only imagine his friends' utterly mismatched standoff.

"Death or capture?" whispered Gnome. A critical decision.

"Death," the friends replied in unison.

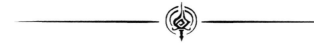

In some unpitying purgatory, X'andria slept fitfully, her nightmares sweaty and touched with terrible visions. Sounds of struggle and impact spiraled and drained into her dream-state. Amidst it all, in the very center, was a bottomless black pit into which she helplessly slipped.

She slowly gained back her awareness. Straining, her open eyes revealed the blurry interior of a devastated rustic dwelling. The noise outside eerily subsided, reduced to the occasional garbled, unintelligible shout. Then her memory came flooding back: they were under siege, and she was probably going to die.

Mind racing and heart pounding, she plunged her cold fingers into her robes and felt a leathery piece of the rotweed that she had found on the roadside what seemed like a lifetime ago. Moving her arm even that much caused excruciating pain in her chest where the arrow had penetrated.

Wincing and tearing up, she staggered to her knees and crawled to the open door. Arden was off to the right, buried in a writhing pile of inky black bonds. Ohlen, Ruprecht and Gnome huddled together, bleeding upon a small battlefield swimming in gore. And she saw a fresh army of hellish bloodthirsty beasts advancing hungrily from the shadows.

It might kill me—but it'll be worth it, if I can save my friends.

X'andria closed her eyes and focused on the crumpled plant matter in her hand. She imagined the army of goblins as they were. She imagined them staggering, struggling for breath, coughing on their knees, tears streaming from their eyes, running for their lives. Then she summoned the word. *Radt-hu'sairk.* Overpower.

Ruprecht, Ohlen and Gnome heard it before they saw it. With the hiss of a huge fireball, X'andria's spell charged past them in a massive roiling grey sphere, gobbling up the distance to the evil army and impacting the earth like a meteor in their midst. An angry swirling grey cloud erupted to consume the entire hoard, and instantly they heard strangled cries and coughing. Goblins scattered in all directions, some fleeing out of sight, some gasping and expiring right there on the ground as they emerged from the expanding haze. The caustic, gaseous grey seared and snaked its way through the clearing invading eyes, noses and mouths. Even as far away as they were standing, X'andria's exhausted friends doubled over coughing, and stumbled back in retreat toward the cottage.

Behind them, X'andria crumbled facedown in a blue-red heap on the ground and lay motionless, the arrow's shaft still protruding defiantly upward toward the rapidly darkening sky.

"X'andria hovers on the edge of this life and the next."

Chapter Ten
SHELTER

"X'an," Gnome spoke urgently, touching his oldest friend's limp shoulder. "X'an, don't give up. We need you." More insistent now, "I need you, X'an. We're going to get you someplace safe. You're going to be alright."

The heinous cloud she had created had been incredibly effective. At least for now. When Gnome went to X'andria's side, Ruprecht and Ohlen raced to Arden to find the black bonds loosening their grip and sagging and dissolving into the ground. Arden painfully extricated himself from the headless goblin he had been imprisoned with, revealing bruises and lacerations where the bonds had disagreed with his attempts to free himself. His right leg was bathed in blood from the arrow, which had since broken near the point of entry.

Chapter Ten

"Just a minute." Arden limped quickly across the lawn to a goblin showing signs of life and drove the point of his forefathers' sword into its neck causing instant stillness. He returned after similarly dispatching several others. "What are we going to do?"

Ohlen spoke gravely, "X'andria hovers on the edge of this life and the next, and we are all weakened and badly injured. The evil will return soon. We need time. And we need luck."

They walked solemnly back to X'andria and Gnome. Gnome was whispering desperately into her unconscious ears, and stroking her thick red hair and knitted forehead.

"Ohlen, Ruprecht, can you help her?" Gnome pleaded. But he already knew the answer. He knew they had called forth their powers to the utmost.

"Arden, I'll pull out the arrow. Can you bind the wound on both sides?" Arden nodded, digging immediately in one of his smaller pouches that held poultices and dressing fabrics. Gnome continued, "And I'll need your field satchel, too. I have an idea."

Removing his hand from her forehead, Gnome gently rolled X'andria onto her side. Grasping the tip of the arrow protruding from her front, he broke the head from the shaft with a grimace. After confirming Arden's readiness, he placed his hand on the flights and pulled the shaft, in one motion, from her torso causing her slight body to convulse with a startled inhalation.

Blood welled instantly, but Arden was a master of field dressing. As Ohlen and Ruprecht looked helplessly on, Arden methodically stemmed the bloodflow with packing and a long strip of fabric tied around X'andria's middle to hold it in place.

The dreaded beasts were returning. Ohlen could feel it, and the others could hear it.

Gnome forced his eyes from X'andria, stood up, and held

Arden's large leather bag before him. "If this works, I need you, Arden, to lift X'andria in first, then climb in yourself, then Ruprecht, then Ohlen. I'll come last."

Rustling in the trees nearby.

Standing tall Gnome stretched the bag wide and held it straight out before him so that the contents nearly spilled out on the ground. The pressure was on. He knew they had less than a minute. He knew they would not survive another encounter with the goblins. Most of all, he knew X'andria was at the edge of death. What he was about to try, he had never before attempted. He'd seen X'andria make one during their studies with The Alchemist, been inside of it, and knew in theory what he was supposed to do.

Another dimension. An invisible room borrowed from another plane. A safe haven. A place they could climb into that no other could find. A transparent womb in which to heal. An opening leading from this world into space borrowed from that one. The word erupted from Gnome, and the mouth of the bag gaped impossibly wide, even as the rest of it disappeared from view. *Gurehm'veilige.* Safety.

Years later it would be a detail he left out. But Gnome, too, fell completely unconscious from the effort involved in creating the safe haven. Ignoring his disbelief, Arden gently placed X'andria, headfirst, into the suspended leather-rimmed maw. Then, after the briefest of hesitations, he dove awkwardly in after her. Gnome was similarly deposited within by Ohlen, though with tremendous difficulty due to Ohlen's fresh shoulder wound.

Goblins came into view just as Ruprecht watched Ohlen's legs disappear into thin air. The beasts shouted as they ran, brandishing a variety of weapons of their own making and of those they had captured. As if trapped in some terrible dream, Ruprecht felt like he moved in slow motion and without strength. He pitched himself forward into the hole, kicking the air with his legs behind him. Arrows whistled past him as he wriggled further in, lower body dangling like some grotesque living target in a shooting range. Ruprecht's feet disappeared within just before they came upon him. Instinctively, he closed together the wide-open lips of the bag behind him.

For otherwise dumb creatures, the Goblins had good tracking skills and an excellent sense of smell, and they were very persistent. For a long time, the lead guard stood staring precisely at the point Ruprecht had vanished, which was, in fact, where they all sat motionless and silent and invisible. In a particularly frightening development, he ordered archers to fire arrows directly at the vanishing point. Arrow after arrow flew straight at the party and then disappeared from view, only to reappear a split second later on the other side of Gnome's otherworldly magic bag. The arrows flew until the two archers lost patience and flung what appeared to be angry protestations at the leader. This led to a violent and bloody brawl between them.

After the goblin arrows and brawl, the friends realized that wherever they were was truly removed from the physical world. While all around them death scoured the ground for their souls, in there they could act without fear of discovery.

They could heal.

For the first time, he was inside the secret room.

Chapter Eleven
TOGETHER

"How long can we stay here?" breathed Ruprecht after it seemed safe to speak.

Gnome, who had regained consciousness, carefully eyed the milling archers around them. "I don't really know. I've never made one of these successfully before."

Ohlen sat awkwardly. Whatever this thing was, it wasn't huge, it had spongy round leathery walls, and he was slouched uncomfortably with nothing firm to adjust against. His shoulder was killing him, and the position he was in had caused the wound to reopen and ooze thick warmth all down his back. It was a very strange sensation to be crammed into a sack with invisible walls suspended in a gaggle of hostile foes. Ohlen's hand rested gently on X'andria's back which was, blessedly, rising and falling in a gentle yet insistent rhythm.

"My only guess is that you've somehow managed to place us in the space between worlds, Gnome," he said thoughtfully. "We all owe our lives to this miracle you have summoned. We owe our lives to you." Ohlen continued, "I surmise, actually, that we may stay here for quite some time. My understanding of this astral space is that it is unfathomably vast and connects all dimensions. I believe it is stable, though. Our only danger here is that another dimensional traveler will stumble upon this tiny corner of the universe. I find that highly unlikely, however."

Arden did not pretend to understand anything Ohlen had just said. "That **thing**," he winced as his fingers dug into his leg in search of the arrowhead and broken shaft, "that tall cretin that shot the wiggly ropes at me..." He sucked in a shuddering breath as he forced extraction of the object from his thigh. Applying heavy pressure with both palms he continued, "...what the hell was that? The stuff hit me harder than I've ever been hit, blew me backward and then snaked around me like it had a life of its own. And any time I'd move or try to get free, it would just get tighter and tighter."

"I've been thinking about that a lot," Ruprecht offered, brown eyes popping open as though he'd just awoken from a daydream. "Rowena said the goblins only came at night, and yet here they were in broad daylight. You all saw how the goblins retreated together and assumed a battle formation with that tall black thing in the middle. It's like it was controlling them."

Several moments passed in silence.

"How's the back?" Arden gestured at Ohlen with a bloody hand, as if offering to examine the wound Ohlen was ignoring. Ohlen indicated X'andria with his eyes, and Arden knew that under no circumstances would Ohlen remove his hand from her body, or move to disturb her in any way.

Ruprecht passed around leathery strips of salted meat and they nibbled quietly. Ohlen paled with each passing minute, though from blood loss or energy drain, they did not know. Gnome allowed Arden to work on his lacerated arms, using the last moments of light to closely observe the movements and tactics of the fell beasts still milling nearby.

Ruprecht retreated into his mindspace.

Unlike Ohlen, who seemed to distill and focus power from the spirits around him and from the ether itself, for Ruprecht elemental transformation was a gift granted from above. He first received the gift in a state of absolute desperation. Many years and many prayers followed before his deity would again return.

The fifth boy in a devoutly religious household, Ruprecht alone showed real interest in his parents' faith. The southern plains, their homeland, were in turmoil under brutal and repressive rule.

It got bad. People were dying, dragged away for questioning and torture. As the great houses warred, the poor who worked the lands paid the price in blood and taxes. Religious devotion was intolerable to those who demanded their serfs worship only themselves. One night his father, long grey hair billowing behind him above his flapping red cloak, flew on horseback to the aid of a captured brother of the faith. He never returned.

Every night at bedtime Ruprecht's mother huddled the children together and blessed them in turn. It was the most loving feeling of his early childhood. There he was, tiny, shivering, and when it was his turn she placed a hand on his little body and murmured things he could not understand with his ears or mind, but which his soul knew to be unconditional love.

The family's altar room was small and secret. Children were not allowed in until after their tenth year. Aware of its existence, they were forbidden ever to mention it, or their faith, to anyone.

At nine, Ruprecht began comprehending the insidiousness of evil. With their father gone, his brothers had lost their way. They joined militias, they fought against friends of the family, they fought against each other, and they abandoned the faith of their childhoods.

In desperation, in the middle of the night, with raiders entering homes and committing atrocities, Ruprecht's mother urgently pulled him from his bed. Even in haste and terror, the warmth of her touch was such that he still remembered it years later—as though it was yesterday. They ventured cautiously downstairs, and she secreted him to the small hidden chamber for the very first time. The door his father, her husband, had expertly crafted to blend seamlessly with the walls, clicked softly closed behind them. Just then the marauding bastards, mostly adolescents not much older than himself, fueled by youthful rage and bloodlust and mass hysteria, came festering into their home like infection from some rotten pustule.

Tears in her resolute and beautiful eyes, his mother lit the huge white candles, and squared his small shoulders to the shabby altar. He was overcome. The horror around them, his mother's love, his father's absence, his brothers' betrayal, and now, for the first time, he was inside the secret room.

It was red. Deeply worn velvety cushions, red walls, a sagging wooden shelf. There were books on the shelf, the candles had dripped wax all over themselves, all over the yellowed pages, on the shelf, on the soft red floor.

TOGETHER

They knelt and they prayed.

His senses expanded outward beyond the red room, beyond the house, beyond the world, into the heavens. What he would later know to be his deity, held him in a state of suspended animation, and suddenly he could see the greedy grins and eager eyes of the invaders in their home, he could see his father's beard and hair and cape all twisted together on a gruesome pile of death, he could see his brothers in their hatred and confusion and guilt and weakness, and, most of all, he could see his mother's love shining like a great golden sun.

And the boy begged. He opened himself up to every vulnerability. He admitted his weakness, he admitted his self-loathing at his own inability to protect anyone and any thing. He laid bare his soul and asked for help.

Help me, god. Please help me. Please protect my mom.

What happened next he would not be able to explain for many, many years. His instructors asked him over and over, and he had no answer. It was like his mind detonated in some sort of explosion of unfathomable might. He saw the villains in and around his home melt like the candles in their secret room. He saw his uncle, miles away, looking straight into his pleading eyes as though they were sitting across a table from one another. He saw his mother, beaming with pride.

The next day they ventured from the secret room to find large gory puddles of men who had been turned inside out strewn throughout their ransacked home. At midday his uncle tore up the path to their home on an enormous and frothing grey steed, with a brown mare tied behind. Shaking off the astonishment on his face at the carnage, his uncle piled them hastily onto the brown, and they galloped off to safety.

Ruprecht would spend the next ten years studying in a small secret guild, he and his mother living under his uncle's watchful and fierce protection. Devoting hours each day to silent prayer, Ruprecht's god finally returned to him one day during a waking nightmare of that terrifying night in the red room. Swirling fear, desperation, love and devotion was his gateway to the divine, and, ever since, recalling the greatest terror and wonder of his life became his daily communion.

The tracks led them deeper into the forest toward the mountains.

Chapter Twelve
ONWARD

They rested and healed overnight in Gnome's astral haven. Dawn brought stormy skies and heavy winds. The rain held off for a few hours but by mid-morning it was positively pouring down from above, drenching the corpses and the muddy, bloody field beneath them.

They felt fortunate, indeed, to be safe and dry while their bodies healed and their minds cleared. And they were elated when, shortly after the rains came, X'andria blearily returned to consciousness, Ohlen's steadying touch still firmly warming her shoulder.

"What happened? Where are we?" she yawned in a sleepy tumble of words, her eyes still closed defiantly.

"X'an!" cried Gnome, "you're awake! How are you feeling?"

Chapter Twelve

"Let's just take it really slowly," warned Ohlen, speaking really slowly himself, as though to illustrate his point.

And it struck them all that Ohlen looked as pale and grey as the billowing clouds above. In actuality he spoke slowly because he lacked the energy to do anything else.

Arden pleaded, "My god, Ohlen, let us take X'andria! Ruprecht," gesturing meaningfully with his eyebrows, "can you help?" Arden was not at all sure what magic people did, or how they accomplished it, but he'd seen enough to know that it was for real.

So the next several hours were spent with Ruprecht praying over Ohlen, while Arden and Gnome watched over X'andria, answered her increasingly insistent questions about the day before, and even ventured a joke or two at meal time in the mid-afternoon. Trading her injury for his own health, it appeared Ohlen had greatly speeded X'andria's recovery, and by dusk her laughter filled their small inter-dimensional space with the light of joy.

"So what's the plan?" asked Gnome, after seeing some color sneaking tentatively back onto Ohlen's face.

"We find them, and we destroy them," declared Arden without hesitation, left hand sneaking toward the ornate pommel of his family's sword.

"What he said," chimed in X'andria, fixing on her business smile, eyes flashing the jade green of her necklace.

"We must go forth immediately," said Ohlen in a resolved monotone. "Our highest priority must be to free and protect any survivors. Time is of the essence."

And so it was. After looking carefully at the perimeter for hostiles, Gnome reopened the magically animated field satchel and slid aside as each of his party climbed back out, and back to earth.

"I must be the last to leave," he explained as they all descended, and, sure enough, the moment his feet hit the ground and his hand left the lip of the bag, Arden's field satchel reappeared in mid-air and then flopped to the ground with a thud. The astral space was no more.

The rains might normally have made tracking difficult, but with the sheer numbers of goblins they were following, Arden was confident that they would be able to pursue the goblins back to wherever they were coming from unless air or water were involved in their movements.

So they walked, Arden in the lead, with Gnome and Ruprecht behind, X'andria fourth, and Ohlen drifting along last. The tracks led them deeper into the forest toward the mountains. They stepped cautiously through the soft wet terrain and were quiet for some time.

"What really happened back there, anyway?" queried X'andria to no one in particular.

"You mean with the bunch of bloodthirsty goblins and that awful rope-slinging creep?" asked Arden conversationally.

"No, I mean, with the hermit," X'andria pressed on, "Rowena seemed to think he possessed some great power, but all we found was a wrecked cottage, and a pretty modest one at that."

They forged ahead silently, X'andria's words fermenting in their minds. They had all, indeed, fixated on the goblins and the prisoners, and the fact that they had found no hermit and instead found days' old, if not weeks' old, destruction with no other clues, had not occupied their thoughts.

The mountains were closer now, and they arrived at a narrow and clear stream that rushed down from higher elevations. Fording it was easy, however, and the wide and messy goblin trail was quickly relocated on the other side.

At dinnertime, they slowed their pace long enough for Gnome to pass around some stale bread and a skin freshly filled with cool mountain water.

"The black orb is immensely potent and harbors an evil will within," intoned Ohlen, as though no time had passed since X'andria's questions about the hermit several hours earlier. Protectively cradling his ivory case through the fabric of his white robes, Ohlen continued, "Try as I may, I cannot put it together in my mind, but I am thoroughly convinced that the hermit's demise and the goblins' treachery are somehow inextricably linked to the orb's dark mystery."

X'andria shivered.

In his heavy chain armor, and with so much of his movement encumbered by bending close to the ground to examine scratches, prints and patterns, Arden's breath became more labored. The grade was rising, too, and soon everyone was feeling the exhaustion from their long day on foot.

Arden slowed, raising his right hand. Gnome grasped his dagger, X'andria extracted a dart from her robe, and Ruprecht found the hilt of his flail. Ohlen, who sensed no presence, merely stopped and awaited the ranger's next move. "We're close now," Arden breathed, "the traffic is heavy, varied, and multidirectional."

The mountain steps began before them. With Arden focused on the ground, Ruprecht, Gnome, and X'andria began scanning the boulders and small cliffs for signs of a cave or passage. Ohlen closed his eyes and invited sensation.

It's funny: once you start looking for an obscure thing in an unfamiliar place, you find evidence of it everywhere. X'andria poked Ruprecht in the ribs through his scratchy brown robes and pointed emphatically at a dark and promising indention, while Gnome, looking off in another direction, whispered "X'an, Ruprecht—does that look like a cave entrance near those shrubs up there?"

But it was Arden whose heavily laden form lurched backward in surprise, finding the entrance to the goblin lair. It was not on the mountain face at all. It was hidden instead in plain sight, perfectly camouflaged under brush, shrubbery and ground cover right in front of them. It was so well-hidden, in fact, that Arden, on all fours, drove his hand straight into the void beneath the thin layer of vegetation, before realizing what he had come upon. Nearly losing his balance with all he carried, he retracted his hand along with a musty, earthy odor laced with a faint reek of sour sweat.

They all noticed Arden's loss of balance and quick recovery. They all knew precisely what he had found.

"Retreat," hissed Gnome, no hint of question or compromise in his voice.

They fell back with Gnome fifty yards or so, Arden instinctively blurring their tracks with light brushing of their prints, using the perimeter of his coiled rope like a great circular paintbrush on the soft wet earth.

At a safe distance, Gnome continued darkly, "we cover our tracks back to the stream. We ford north five hundred paces and, if Arden sees no signs of goblin traffic, we'll rest a few hours. Then we'll invade that accursed hole, visit misery upon these savages, and bring Arden's people back home."

It was about twenty feet before the earth leveled off into a tunnel before them, with room enough only for single file.

Chapter Thirteen
INTO THE FRAY

─────────────

Arden's had been the first watch of the evening, after which he plunged into a fitful, troubled sleep. He dreamt of gnashing teeth, of howling winds and howling wolves, and of barbarian blades that seemed impossibly huge to his four-year-old eyes as they slashed through all he knew and loved. These were Arden's earliest memories.

His parents traveled in a small group through the wilderness. They walked and gathered and hunted during the days and camped in the nights. He did not know who slaughtered them all, but the feelings of fear and helplessness that gripped his young soul that bleak fateful night would never let him go. For a few years they caused him to withdraw silently into the thoughtful, watchful world of his childhood.

Chapter Thirteen

Later they would drive him to strengthen his body, sharpen his mind, hone his senses, and ultimately commit to a life of virtue.

He heard the men sneaking into camp and awoke just in time to witness the horrific attacks. His mother and father lamely tried to cover him with bags and bedding, but quickly were drawn away weeping and shrieking in their futile attempts to defend themselves.

Then came the wolves. Three huge black wolves with enormous fangs and glowing eyes charged into the clearing. Peering out from beneath his blankets, Arden saw the first one, in full flight, stretched eight feet nose to tail, hurtling through the air to clamp its massive jaws on the face and throat of his mother's murderer. That man's body went rigid as he stumbled backward and brought his hands up to find the mutilation that had been his face.

Arden's last memories of that night were of a still and silent camp in which everyone he knew had perished at the hands of merciless bandits, of bandits who had themselves been destroyed by otherworldly beautiful and terrible beasts, and of one of those beast's glowing eyes boring into his own so close he could feel its burning breath on his glistening cheeks.

He was found, the next day, by a gentle and loving man who raised him in the forest as his own son. Though Arden said very few words as a boy, the man showered him with his knowledge of flora and fauna and the animal world around them. On they day they chose as his tenth birthday, Arden's adoptive father presented him with a magnificent sword—Arden's family weapon—he explained that he'd found it in the camp the morning after Arden's parents had been murdered. As Arden grew and showed interest in strength and combat, his new father taught him all he knew of swordplay, and was even a good sport for grueling practices long after Arden had surpassed the man's abilities with a blade. Each night Arden found himself straining to hear the howling of wolves, and, once in a while, he was rewarded with the far off echoes of their haunting songs.

Arden woke with a start. Sweating, he turned noiselessly to scan his party's small camp in the moonlight. His dream world slowly faded and he could see that Ohlen was sitting alert at the perimeter watching over them with his ethereal serenity. Arden could see all was as it should be. And he smiled, and he allowed himself to slip back into his memories.

It was not until his sixteenth year that his adoptive father finally admitted, "I have something to share with you, son, and I need you to sit down."

Arden sat warily on their heavy oak bench. The man continued, "I have kept something secret from you all these years, but I think now is the time you should know." He continued on gravely, "Before I do, though, I want you to know that I love you. You are my only son. You have grown to be a strong and courageous man, and I could not be more proud."

And with that his dad sat calmly on the floor, looking straight into his eyes.

A moment later his father's face turned rigid and the bones of his upper jaw and nose had somehow detached inside and were being forced forward with unstoppable power into the painfully stretched skin of his face. His back arched and his torso pitched forward with a violent jerk—he kept himself from falling onto his misshapen face by sticking his hands out before him on the wooden floor. Except his hands were no longer hands at all. They were, instead, massive claws with flesh boiling in a rush to become black fur over compact wolf paws.

Through it all, his eyes never left Arden. Arden had always known there was something familiar in his father's gaze. The realization that his father was, in fact, the wolf who had saved his life, only deepened his love and gratitude.

Tears streaming from his eyes, he fell to his knees and locked his dad in a long and powerful embrace, his hands buried in the thick wolf fur.

"It's time to go," announced Gnome a few minutes later in a loud whisper. They had risen in the moonlight, eaten, and were mostly packed up.

"Before we go into the fray," said Ruprecht softly with outstretched arms, "let us strengthen our spirits."

They huddled together then, X'andria, Ohlen, Gnome and Arden, to receive Ruprecht's blessing.

It was strange this time. Easier. Like Ruprecht's deity was leading him, encouraging him, guiding him. And he walked into the blinding light not as one humble soul cowering before its brilliance, but together with his companions, as though they were all welcomed for this one special moment. *Safety, strength, and justice.* Those were his noble requests.

We go tonight, god, to face powers great and terrible. We go into the den of evil. Bless us, I pray, in our efforts to do good in this world.

They crept back to the goblin lair. Arden was first, then Gnome, X'andria, Ruprecht and Ohlen. After removing the camouflage around the entrance and hearing no movement within, they stepped and slipped carefully down the steep, pebbly hole. After twenty feet, the earth leveled off into a tunnel before them, with room enough only for single file.

There was a stifling odor here. Far more pungent than the dank stagnant air of underground, this was mixed also with the smell of unclean musky bodies crammed together with no ventilation. X'andria had once crossed the sea in a lower hold. This, she reflected glumly, smelled like that dreaded space.

Torchlight. About fifty feet or so into the tunnel, after the moon's faint glow behind them had faded entirely, an orange light flickered in the distance. Arden halted the party. Still no sound.

Gnome and X'andria both moved soundlessly. With a faint gesture from Arden, Gnome knew it was time to scout ahead. Moments later he returned.

"The tunnel splits, there's a torch, nothing more."

They descended. Arden, Ohlen, and Ruprecht found themselves having to stoop low to avoid hitting their heads on the damp and dirty ceiling. X'andria thumbed her darts nervously.

They went to the right. It was still curiously quiet. Ohlen treaded carefully backward to ensure they would not be surprised from behind.

In the wall was a heavy, rusty, sweaty iron door. It was set in a frame of the same material, and sunk at a slight angle into the earth. A guttering torch fluttered nearby. Gnome examined the hardware closely. Satisfied that they were not being followed, Ohlen, too, turned his attention to the door, laying his hand on the cold damp metal.

"Fear," Ohlen whispered. "It should open, Arden," concluded Gnome.

Chapter Thirteen

With a creak louder than they would have liked, Arden opened the door.

It was a hole more than a room. Rats scattered to the periphery. It smelled horrendous. Creeping carefully inside, Arden's boots met heavy clinking metal objects amongst an array of what looked like fragments of leather and fabric in the dirt. X'andria's sensitive nose brought her to suspicious masses, some of which might have been moldy food, while others were most certainly excrement. "Chains and restraints," sighed Gnome, locating a buried set of iron manacles.

"This must be a holding cell for their prisoners," observed Ruprecht, feeling sick. He tightly closed his eyes, lips working in silent prayer.

Leaving the cell, Arden's pace began to quicken. They all knew that time was not on their side if they wanted to find and liberate the abducted unfortunates of Westover. Following his lead, they backtracked to the fork in the tunnel and proceeded down the left path instead. Gnome's legs pumped back and forth quickly just to keep up, though his early life had been underground, and here he moved like a fish in the sea.

Suddenly they heard sounds of movement and shouting in the distance.

Arden began to run, steel flashing in his hand.

Something that made him think the gods had, perhaps,
not forgotten him after all.

Chapter Fourteen
WINE AND CHEESE

I am not forsaken!

Many hours had passed since his escape. Boudreaux stalked the dark halls, stopping to listen at regular intervals. It was slow going. His odor continued to be an advantage, since it seemed to draw the foul beasts to him in groups of two or three at a time. He came upon several hollowed-out rooms, one of which contained four of the creatures snoring loudly, at least until about ten seconds after his arrival.

In all Boudreaux had quietly slain about a dozen pig men—or were they female, he couldn't tell. He dragged each of them down to the growing pile of bodies near the dungeon, before stealthily advancing back through the dim tunnels. Only one had made significant noise before being permanently silenced, and that had attracted the attention of several others nearby. Boudreaux was thankful no more had been in range of hearing.

He now had a small collection of poorly-made weapons, but some weapons were certainly better than none.

It was on his tenth trip out that he discovered the casks of wine. Something that made him think the gods had, perhaps, not forgotten him after all.

There was food too. Small salted and dried carcasses that might have been rats or squirrels hung over bags and crates stamped with ornate lettering that were spoils of war, for the packages and their contents had most certainly not been produced by these savages.

The cheese was magnificent. One crate contained a wheel of creamy white and Boudreaux knew it would take tremendous self-control not to gorge himself on the entire thing. He was so committed to slowing himself down on the cheese that he poked a large hole in the top of one of the wine casks with his spear and took a long and luxurious drink of the glorious ruby red liquid. *Delicious.*

He sat on a crate and thought about Phase Two.

He had been efficient. He had gone unnoticed. He had amassed a small collection of weapons and now, just as importantly, he had located a store of food and drink.

The problem with Phase Two was that it involved people. Boudreaux was a loner. He worked best by himself and found that others tended to get in the way, slow things down, cause distraction, and oftentimes ruin everything through sheer stupidity and ineptitude. Through all his disdain for partnership, though, he actually had a huge soft spot for kind and gentle people. That made things even worse in battle, because he found himself compromising his tactics to protect the innocents present.

After softly closing the door to the storeroom and listening for activity, Boudreaux snuck cautiously back down the twisting and deserted passageways to the dungeon with a wheel of cheese and a cask of wine under his left arm, and his trusty spear in his right hand. With the wine and cheese deposited on the ground, he grabbed a small axe from his pile of weapons, pulled a torch from the wall, and gently pushed open the door to the dungeon.

Ugh, it smells horrible. It was easy to forget how terrible the odor was after even a short while in the relatively fresh air of the tunnels. Standing in the forlorn space with torchlight, Boudreaux was horrified at the condition of the prisoners. Some were passed out, or sleeping; some were most certainly dead. Those that were awake seemed too stunned or crazed to register the meaning of his presence.

"We're getting out of here, and I need help," he announced in his most business-like manner. "Who can stand with me?"

Blank stares.

Blank stares were just fine, actually. Boudreaux made a quick mental list of the eight individuals who looked most alert. He was privately delighted to see that the girl he had accompanied here was among those closely watching him. With one well-placed powerful strike of his axe he swiftly opened each cage in turn, held the doors wide, and demanded his chosen helpers step out to join him.

Those too weak or too witless to move, will have to endure this hell for just a little longer.

Once outside, he offered his dazed companions the wine and cheese he had brought from the storeroom. It did not take long for their confusion and disbelief to turn into hunger and thirst and eagerness and fear.

Then, standing in a huddled and shivering circle, with bits of cheese on their hands and on the ground, and wine staining their parched lips, Boudreaux told them his plan.

Boudreaux stripped off all the metal objects he could find.

Chapter Fifteen
BOUDREAUX'S PLAN

"Everyone lives," Boudreaux eyed each of the dirty prisoners intently. "That's our primary objective." The boy from Boudreaux's first night down here groped for more cheese without removing his eyes from the stout and powerful half elf.

"To do that will require many things, the most important of which is that you do exactly as I say." Silence. Boudreaux took that to be tacit agreement.

And silent agreement was a good thing, too, because at that precise moment, Boudreaux's sharp ears picked up the faint sound of a few sets of boots running hurriedly toward them from around the bend in the tunnel.

"Excuse me for a moment," Boudreaux breathed. Then he added unnecessarily, "Stay quiet."

Huddled together they watched the mysterious half-dressed man—he had a small breast plate strapped low on his front mostly covering his nether parts, but his back side was entirely bare—glide silently to the corner and peer around. A moment later, when they, too, heard the rushing of feet toward them, he shot around the corner out of sight with astonishing speed. There was less of a collision than they expected, between his speedy departure and the hasty gait of the oncoming intruders. What they heard instead were liquidy squelches, muted cracking sounds, a snort, and several dull thuds.

Moments later the man returned carrying two of their fiendish piggy tormentors hanging lifeless, one in each arm. He walked purposely past them and deposited the bodies atop a pile of the dozen others. It was the first time they had noticed the pile of bodies in the darkness of the tunnel, and it was the first time they each felt hope since their capture, what seemed like a lifetime ago.

They would do anything for this man.

Boudreaux divided them into two teams of four: fortifiers and distributors. The fortifiers were to drag the dead bodies to two predetermined points along the network of tunnels and stack them into defensive walls. These walls, according to the man who called himself Boudreaux, would not only form protective barriers for those behind them, but would also intimidate the enemy. The fortifiers were to begin immediately. Once the walls were built, they were to arm themselves and remain, two by two, behind their walls until further instructions.

The distributors received their instructions in soft hurried bursts as they followed Boudreaux to the storeroom. Their job was complex. Retrieve all the healthy food from the storeroom and return it to the dungeon, come two at a time back to the storeroom to collect any freshly deposited bodies, weapons, armor, or other useful material. Dole out the food, weapons and other supplies using good judgment. Stay armed at all times. Never travel alone.

As the other three distributors entered the storeroom to load their skinny arms with food and drink, Boudreaux held the girl, Helga, back for an extra word.

"Helga, I have a job of critical importance for you." Helga's huge and deep blue eyes focused piercingly on his own. "You must recruit and train other able-bodied prisoners to help us. Return to the dungeon, calm them, and encourage them. Those with clear minds need to follow you out of their cages where you will feed them, explain our situation, and assign them their duties. This is important, but also very dangerous, for under no circumstances can any of our group be allowed to advance forward to the fighting. If they do, I cannot guarantee their safety, and they will most assuredly perish. Do you understand?" Helga understood, and raced to fill her own small arms with a crate and to catch up with the others, who were already on their way back toward the dungeon.

Some time later, when she and the others crept cautiously back to the storeroom along the dank and eerily quiet tunnels, the only signs of their benefactor were three freshly deposited corpses across the entrance.

Boudreaux now had a problem. The tunnel split. No matter which direction he chose he would leave himself open to ambush from behind or, worse, the possibility of the hellish piggy bastards wandering down to face the hopelessly underprepared gaggle he had left by the dungeon.

Time to wait. Time to listen. Time to think.

Three of the squat creatures came bustling hurriedly down the right tunnel barking animated comments at one another in their aggressive guttural language. *I wonder if they now know?* They knew. For instead of walking confidently in the direction of the dungeon, toward Boudreaux, they stopped and quieted. Small swords drawn, they advanced with predatory menace in their darting black eyes, their wide wet nostrils flaring.

It was a short fight, but a much better challenge than any he'd faced so far. They were ready, they were on alert, and while they did not come close to landing any blows, Boudreaux had to be considerably more calculating in his approach. They were aggressive fighters, not inclined to wait for their opponent to move. Their early commitment was a huge weakness, however, because their clumsy movements, though laced with deadly intent, were slow and easy to read.

The first assailant charged him with a squeal, raising his sword as he came. Boudreaux's long spear caught him just under his throat, where he was skewered by his own propulsion. The sword, though, was still arcing dangerously forward and Boudreaux had to move quickly in order to avoid its trajectory. Still holding the spear, he sprung to the right and used the long handle to parry the next assailant's strike, jerking and spinning the first stuck beast by the head as he moved, who gurgled to his death at the other end.

The force of the parry sent the second attacker's blade clattering to the ground, and the attacker itself staggering awkwardly forward right into Boudreaux. Dropping the spear handle Boudreaux thrust two thick fingers of his left hand directly into the creature's eyes while lifting it from the ground with his right hand under its armpit. It blubbered and clawed wildly and Boudreaux threw it violently at the bewildered third. The resulting dazed tangle of limbs on the ground was quickly silenced.

Breathing heavily now, an idea came creeping into his mind. Boudreaux stripped off all the metal objects he could find, the swords, the various armor plates, and a helmet. Walking about fifteen feet down the tunnel, he began stacking all the pieces into a precariously balanced tower. It was too far for anyone to see from the junction, but close enough that if anything came that way and accidentally nudged the tower, he'd be likely to hear the resulting crash.

Satisfied with his precautionary measure, he deposited the bodies at the storeroom and returned to the split in the tunnel.

Another hour or so passed. Gaining confidence as he memorized the pathways and learned more and more of their combat techniques, Boudreaux prowled through the halls like a hunter in a jungle teeming with prey. The right fork had divided into a series of honeycomb nests where, perhaps, these things ate and bred and slept. It was warmer and the stench was unbearable. He encountered the stiffest resistance yet in this place, and took several minor blows that were bothersome but not critical. Thankfully, though, on his final trip into the nests, he discovered that there was no other outlet. This meant he could advance confidently down the left fork without fear that his line would be breached.

And that's when he heard it.

His metal tower crashed in the distance. Heart pounding, Boudreaux raced at top speed back to the junction and sped toward the dungeon and his wards. Passing the fallen tower he stopped dead in his tracks. Helga was standing before him in the middle of the tunnel, her huge eyes brimming with tears.

"I told him not to go," she stammered, the only words he had heard her speak beyond her name. "He wouldn't listen. He just ran. I'm s-so sorry." Her small shoulders slumped.

"Not your fault, Helga. Get them battle-ready," he ground out, spun around, and sprinted back down the hall, his heart in his mouth.

Must've gone left, I was right.

Flying around the corner, no time for stealth.

I knew it. This could easily be it.

Snap judgments, passing a tunnel mouth to the right, a startled beast squealing and pointing as he blurred by.

What would I do, where would I go, if I were a crazed imbecile trying to get out?

They were coming behind him. They were calling, they were grunting, shrieking, the numbers were growing. More tunnels, more wild guesses.

Where could this idiot be?

And then he found him. It was the old man who had been chained behind him on their first day in this hell hole. His eyes were crazed, he had a tortured grimace plastered on his face, his naked body was smeared from the unspeakable muck of his imprisonment, and he was pinned by spears to the wall of the tunnel in three places by gleeful and eager slobbering pig men.

Rage is a remarkable thing. With its potent venom coursing through his body, Boudreaux obliterated the three murderers in an explosion of force. He hit their startled faces so hard that his fists sank into their skulls before impact caught up with their bodies and blew them backward in messy heaps.

Without even looking at the advancing hoards behind him,

BOUDREAUX'S PLAN

Boudreaux extracted the three spears pinning the wretched lifeless soul to the wall, spun, and launched them in quick succession at the encroaching crush of death. The force of their launch, and the density of the angry mob, caused each spear to plow two or three deep into the oncoming beasts. Boudreaux drew a short sword, his jaw set.

Ten down, a hundred to go.

It was a large room, the largest he had seen in the underground network apart from the confounding hall of the dwarves. Tunnels entered from several directions, and the hideous things flowed from each of them like copious waste into a sewer main.

I'm going to die here. I will take some with me, but I cannot take them all.

I failed you Helga, you smart, sweet girl. I am so sorry.

He stumbled and slipped on gore and goblin parts beneath him.

Chapter Sixteen
DEEPER IN

They all heard the commotion in the distance. Ohlen sensed the strength of Arden's resolve and the surge of his valor just moments before the big man sprang forward toward the sounds.

And so it begins.

Gnome darted like a shadow behind Arden, his superior reaction time never ceasing to amaze. X'andria and Ruprecht fell in behind with their long easy gaits, X'andria loading darts into her left hand in anticipation of battle. Ohlen, as always, watched from the rear.

They passed deserted hallways. The tunnel became larger, twisting and turning and plunging ever deeper into the black earth. Arden's pace did not slow until the tunnel split wide open to reveal a large, dark cavern.

It was warm here, with a sticky stifling smell. There was a

palpable hazy odor, as if the space had just moments before been occupied by a dense sweaty crowd that had somehow vanished the very instant they raced in.

The terrain was filthy and uneven. Shelves of dirt and rock, worn paths, and roughly dug holes of various sizes were covered with refuse and detritus. In a far corner coals glowed beneath what appeared to be a massive smelting apparatus that belched acrid fumes. It was clearly a busy common area, and, with only a quick scan, Ohlen could see the network of paths led to a variety of tunnels thrusting outward at odd angles and elevations.

From the lowest of the departing passageways, on the far side of the chamber, violent and tumultuous sounds emanated, indicating to where the beasts had fled.

Arden was halfway across the room already, advancing more slowly and silently now, like a predator, Gnome on his left flank. The others joined them, and they proceeded cautiously toward the unknown.

The scene they came upon was like none they had ever witnessed. There were so many goblins that the room seemed to be swimming with them, a maniacal school of fish caught in a giant whirlpool. The convergence point was just in front of a bloody, emaciated old man completely naked and crumpled by the cavern wall, his limbs askew and motionless.

Arden's adrenaline-soaked nerves strained against his taut frame. Only Gnome's hand, placed firmly on Arden's right arm, steadied the man as they took stock of the hellish scene.

Then the crush of goblins at the center of the vortex exploded outward like dry leaves hit by a sudden blast of wind. With a roar, a red glistening figure was momentarily exposed within. He stumbled and slipped on gore and goblin parts beneath him, and he yelled crazed and incomprehensible taunts as he was again completely obscured by a fresh wave of clawing and biting beasts.

Arden was off. He was a thing of terrible beauty to behold as his blades cut, lightning fast, into the backs of the nearest goblins who would never know what slew them. Gnome was just behind, his dagger flashing savagely at any living thing that Arden, in his haste to reach the embattled warrior, left standing.

Time to go.

Ohlen was running. He was drawing his sword. He parried, he struck, he defended, he attacked. But his real battle was internal now. Even as he fought by Gnome and Arden, Ohlen focused inwardly on the malevolence pressing around them.

It was suffocating. They were engulfed by malice of inestimable magnitude. It might have been too much for him had he not had his friends' light from which to draw strength. Arden and Gnome before him, X'andria and Ruprecht at the perimeter, and a strong but dreadfully injured aura shining dimly from the mysterious warrior. These were strength and resilience and goodness. These were his companions, and while he could not overcome the overwhelming wave of hatred surrounding them, he was able to form a powerful alliance of their wills that melted at least the nearest blackness.

Ohlen's powerful aura repelled their closest assailants, and they cut nearer and nearer to the smothered fighter. Goblins came from all sides, however, and Gnome was now forced to shield his left arm that had been crushed by a well-aimed club. Ohlen had nicks all over his arms, and one particularly nasty slice along the back of his right leg that was now slick with blood. If he had been injured, Arden certainly showed no sign of it as his blades whirred with mesmerizing speed and deadly accuracy, somehow so methodical and efficient as to appear effortless.

Chapter Sixteen

With so many assailants, X'andria and Ruprecht quickly agreed he should pray for assistance from his god. Her job was to buy him time.

X'andria and Ruprecht hugged the wall. They watched as their companions felled dozens of beasts. On several occasions, the mysterious man—if that's what he was—had managed to throw off piles of goblins with tremendous force, but eventually he'd gone silent and invisible under the squirming mass.

With Arden, Ohlen and Gnome ferociously engaging the beasts, X'andria and Ruprecht did not attract very much attention along the perimeter, but any attention was more than they wanted. X'andria was quick to fire off darts at the snarling faces of any beasts that ventured near.

The minute or so that Ruprecht stopped and silently prayed crept by like an eternity. The chaos and danger surrounding them was fuel for his communion. Moments later Ruprecht fell sweating and swaying to his knees, crocus petals spilling from his seizing fists.

"Sleep, my lord. Bring me deep impenetrable sleep to shroud this cruel savage mass in unconscious stillness." *The goblins were too many. He was asking too much. Ruprecht's body shook. His deity towered before him, unimaginably vast. Oily black smoke poured forth and snaked all around him, engulfing him. So much power. So much dream-laced darkness. Far away, in his body, he knew vessels were bursting in his nose and in his eyes as he tried to drink up the phenomenal power he was being offered. I must close their hate-filled eyes. Still their evil minds.*

Ruprecht's bloodshot eyes flew open. Night-black fog seeped heavily out through his nose and mouth, slowly at first, and fell heavily around him in dark, thick pools. It flooded, more quickly now, around X'andria's ankles and raced toward the battle, little tendrils snaking and smoking their way toward the goblin combatants.

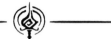

He looked really, really bad. Arden, Ohlen, and Gnome had fought their way to the fallen fighter and formed a shield around him, lashing out at anything that came near with what was left of their strength. The man lay face down in the muck, his body so sliced and so clawed and so completely saturated in blood that it was impossible to tell which parts were him, and which were not. Motionless, he was probably dead or dying.

Though they had many questions about the man, the answers would have to wait. Encircled by dozens of menacing goblins, the warriors were wounded, they were exhausted, and their best hope was that, standing together, their sheer skill and resolve would protect them before any more of the fiends' reinforcements clambered into the engagement.

At that moment goblins began to drop one by one. Ohlen was the first to notice the smoky black fingers creeping up the round bodies, snaking around their blotchy stout necks, and seeping into their mouths and snouts and hairy ears. Soon Arden and Gnome saw it too, and realized a silent river of black was flowing from Ruprecht's face at the edge of the cavern, and causing their attackers to teeter and drop heavily to the ground.

This turn of events gave Arden, Gnome and Ohlen new inspiration, and they focused their wrath on the few goblins still engaging them. In a short while, it was unexpectedly, eerily quiet.

"They're sleeping!" exclaimed X'andria in a loud whisper. "Ruprecht put them to sleep." Ruprecht, no longer belching the heavy black river of sleep, slumped pallid and lifeless like he was about to vomit.

Sleep, Arden and Gnome decided with a quick look at one another, was not good enough, and they set about the grim task of making sure the slumbering goblins strewn throughout the carnage would never wake up. From their still targets, X'andria plucked, cleaned and stowed all the heavy, barbed darts she could spot.

Ohlen grasped under the arms of the heavy, slippery warrior. On closer examination he appeared to be some kind of elf, though bulkier and more square-featured than any elf Ohlen had encountered before. Ohlen began to drag him over to where Ruprecht was seated, away from the gore.

My, how this one has suffered.

Dragging him was not easy. He was exceptionally heavy, the ground was slick, and Ohlen's wounded leg complained bitterly at the effort and the awkward angles.

He is alive. His spirit fights.

Ohlen stopped to adjust his grip. Every inch of the man was bloody, but at least it was congealing and drying. He managed ten more backward steps. Ohlen felt dark presences being extinguished from the ether as Arden and Gnome dispatched the last of the sleeping goblins. More steps. Ohlen had now dragged the enormous elf past the crooked naked corpse of the old man by the wall.

Just a few more steps.

The arrow hit Ohlen in the right clavicle. Since he was bent over the unconscious warrior at the point of impact, it entered the top of his torso and bit deep into his chest cavity from above. He'd been dragging with all his might, but the shock and piercing pain caused him to immediately lose his grip, which resulted in him launching backward, wildly out of control. He did manage to see the archer, hiding in the mouth of a tunnel on the near side of the large chamber, busily notching another arrow.

Ohlen landed hard on his back and his head smacked painfully on the compact floor. But nothing, not the arrow in his body, not the shock of being hit, not the fall, not the carnage, not the exhaustion—nothing compared to the blinding assault on his brain that screeched into his consciousness when the ivory case that held the black marble came tumbling out of his pocket and snapped open on the ground behind him.

It was as if hell itself had been unleashed just feet away from him. And it was angry. It was angry about being locked up. Angry at Ohlen.

Twisting painfully on the ground, the shaft of the arrow grating against the inside of his ribcage, Ohlen strained to retrieve his ivory case.

But by the time he turned over, he saw that the situation was worse than he imagined: far, far worse.

The marble was rolling right to Ruprecht, kneeling catatonic on the ground, with bloodshot eyes and traces of red at his nostrils. Ohlen screamed with the agony of realization just as the marble came to rest at the tip of Ruprecht's left ring finger.

The effect was instantaneous.

A thousand tiny barbed needles burst out of the marble. It seized his finger and thrust itself directly into his flesh under his skin. Ohlen watched in impotent horror as the marble buried itself aggressively inside Ruprecht's ruptured hand. It then began to travel beneath the skin past his wrist and up his arm. Under the skin it appeared to be a round lump covered with flailing tendrils that propelled forward, leaving a large dark purplish river of destruction in its wake.

Ruprecht's body was gripped by convulsions. It seemed a long time before he stopped screaming. Eventually his body stilled. When at last he opened his eyes, they were orbs of jet black.

And there was the unstoppable destruction of the orb tearing through muscles and tendons as it burrowed through his impotent arm toward his shoulder and chest.

Chapter Seventeen
INTO THE BLACK

Complete loss of control. The pain—indescribable. His fingertip was torn open, flayed by the violent invasion of a fiery darkness.

But there was nothing he could do.

While corporeal pain blinded Ruprecht's senses, at the same time he was somewhere outside his body, watching a breach he was powerless to stop.

Where was he?

This thing had turned his hand into jelly. It was moving through his wrist.

Oh god, make it stop! Maybe once it's fully embedded, it will be satisfied.

It was not satisfied.

As sure as Ruprecht knew his own name, he knew that the marble would never be satisfied. It was plowing forward, eating its way up his arm, when Ruprecht felt the eyes for the first time.

Utter domination. The gaze that now pinned him belonged to evil incarnate. Its hunger was so vast it could never be sated. No sustenance could fill this void.

And darkness began to spread. He realized, suddenly, that he was in the little room. The secret room his father and mother had made. The room where he had first experienced god. He knelt there, in the red, his terrified little body shivering in the cold. But his mother was not beside him. His deity did not tower before him with benevolent might this time.

No. Search as he might, his deity was nowhere to be found. Instead there was the pressing insistent fury of the eyes. And there was the unstoppable destruction of the orb tearing through muscles and tendons as it burrowed through his impotent arm toward his shoulder and chest. There was insatiable, crushing desire. Desire to own and enslave, control and dominate.

What was it? Was he the one to be dominated? Yes. He was the conquest.

Or was it his own desire he felt expanding within him? His own lust for power?

Hungry, fiery eyes came rushing to him through his mindspace. The red room splintered and fell away. He was spinning now. He was falling. He was laughing.

They were not another's eyes after all. These were his eyes. So Ruprecht opened them wide, and all of a sudden, his world became crystal clear.

The tunnel plunged. This was a far steeper grade
than the other passages.

Chapter Eighteen
RETREAT

"We gotta go," insisted Gnome. "Arden, take the big man. We have about thirty seconds, I'd guess. Let's get the hell out of here."

Arden and Gnome had rushed the goblin archer. Between them his ending was swift and efficient, and they had returned to the others.

"Seriously folks," Gnome whispered urgently, Arden had already hoisted up the embattled warrior. "Move right now or we'll be goblin feed."

Gnome's insistence faltered. He was now aware of Ruprecht's

inhuman stare, blood streaming from his left hand, and of Ohlen and X'andria's stupefied horror.

But he didn't falter long. "X'an, I don't know what went down here, but if we all die right now, I'll never get to find out. Ohlen, snap out of it!" He swatted Ohlen, hard, on the leg.

More were coming. It sounded like an army stamping, swarming in the distance, echoing through the halls.

"I'll get Ruprecht," murmured Ohlen, focused entirely on his friend's unblinking black eyes.

"*Now* X'an," Gnome was pleading "Let's move! Arden, back the way we came, fast as you can, follow my lead."

Goblins were drawing near. They distinctly heard the savage shouting, the rushing of boots on the packed earth, and the clanging of metal.

Gnome ran. Arden lumbered behind with the massive sticky body in his arms. X'andria tore her eyes from Ruprecht, where he knelt stricken and prone on the ground. The dainty crocus petals before him made a cruel contrast with the gore from his mutilated hand that now stained his simple brown robes. X'andria faltered backward a few steps before turning to hasten after the others.

This left only two.

"Ruprecht?"

Ohlen advanced awkwardly to his friend, the arrow shaft piercing down into his chest cavity making movement extremely difficult. Ruprecht made no move and took no notice. Nothing registered at all, like he was a statue.

Ohlen touched Ruprecht's shoulder.

His friend's body seemingly exploded from the inside with a spiritual force so wicked that Ohlen was blown backward into unconscious oblivion. The last thing he perceived was a hideous black abyss striking serpentine out of Ruprecht's sightless eyes at his very soul.

X'andria cried out. Fleeing, she had taken a last look over her shoulder, and she witnessed the touch. She saw Ohlen's body blown through the air like a doll. Ruprecht stood mechanically and walked stiffly in the opposite direction away from them, heedless of X'andria's desperate plea. Arden, having heard, pounded up behind her.

"He's... a monster." She managed.

"Help Gnome with the big guy. Run!" Arden shouted, racing to the sprawling Ohlen. The goblin hoard was moments away.

Hastily dragging the stranger by his legs, X'andria and Gnome stumbled backward into the large adjacent common room. Arden piled in next to them. It looked as though Ohlen, clutched awkwardly, might spill from his grasp at any moment. They lingered only long enough to switch burdens, Arden once again picking up the large stranger so that Gnome and X'andria could strain at the shoulders and feet of the unconscious Ohlen. From their vantage point, they had just enough time to see goblins streaming into the blood-soaked cavern behind them, saw them investigating their many fallen, completely ignoring Ruprecht striding tall and purposefully in their midst.

"This way," breathed Arden heavily, heading toward a dark tunnel low and to the left. "When we came through earlier, I saw this way was the least traveled." Gnome and X'andria staggered behind. "Maybe we can hide here awhile."

"Maybe," Gnome was panting, "there's something worse," pant, "than goblins down there."

The tunnel plunged. This was a far steeper grade than the other passages. They slowed their pace. Exhaustion was catching up with

Chapter Eighteen

them. Their heavy loads seemed to weigh more with every step. Arden could not see well in this black. X'andria could see somewhat, but only Gnome had faultless intuition underground. Though they did not hear sounds ahead or behind, they dared not risk a torch.

"Hang on, Arden," Gnome whispered. "We'll lead, follow our sound." They pushed awkwardly past one another, hoisting and squeezing their live cargo in the cramped tunnel, and continued on more cautiously.

It was becoming colder. Wetter. "There is stone above us," said Gnome, he could feel it. "It's heavy, dense, cold. This tunnel is burrowing beneath it, that's why we've been going down so fast. Whoever dug this tunnel was trying to get under the rock."

Arden slipped and fell. The stranger landed heavily on top of him. Arden was so weary, cold, hungry, hurting—but there was no time to rest. He forced his reluctant muscles to respond, stood and hoisted the huge awkward burden back into his heavy arms, and on they went.

Gnome's feet hit mud. He was not expecting it. His foot landed harder than normal, carrying half of Ohlen's weight, and it slid quickly in the slick goop. He fell hard and fast, Ohlen toppling behind him, bringing down X'andria as well. Arden, unable to stop, tripped over them and flew forward, pitching himself, and the stranger, into a shallow and frigid pool of water with a splash.

Breathing, deep and fast, is all you hear when scurrying madly in silence. Gnome and X'andria scuttled backward on their behinds, pulling Ohlen's dead weight with them. Arden extracted the stranger from the water with some difficulty, and slipped and staggered his way back to dry land.

And they listened, shivering.

Silence. Not even distant sound. Nothing coming from the

water before them.

"Light?" asked Arden, blade in hand.

X'andria silently rummaged in her small backpack for tinder and her travel torch. Moments later, light sputtered meekly to life in her hands, before gaining confidence and growing to illuminate the space around them.

X'andria's eyebrows came together as she gazed at the stone wall across the pool. Is that what I think it is?

Chapter Nineteen
THE WALL

A stone wall. They had expected many things, but among them was not a hand-crafted stone wall stretching across the tunnel just past the small stagnant pool they'd fallen in moments before.

The stranger moaned; perhaps the icy water had cut through to his consciousness.

The black earthen tunnel with its slick and slimy walls narrowed around them. As far as they could tell it terminated here in this pool of stagnant water against the massive and mysterious wall.

They could see each other now, and they looked awful. Haggard and dirty and cold and wet, X'andria was the only one who was not also bruised and bloody.

Another tortured moan escaped the stranger's crusted lips. His body was covered in lacerations, like his skin was constructed of loosely arrayed pieces of fabric the seamstress had yet to sew together.

"Something to eat?" X'andria queried, fishing in her bag for her small store of dry meat and bread.

Arden and Gnome gratefully accepted what she offered and they munched slowly in silence. Chewing the dry food was hard and swallowing was harder, but with enough time their saliva began to flow and their nutrient-starved bodies began to feel like themselves again.

Arden produced a skin of water and they each took a small sip to help wash down their modest meal. X'andria carefully splashed a small swig into the stranger's mouth, whose cracked lips drank up the liquid like dry earth.

"What the hell happened to Ruprecht?" asked Gnome bitterly.

"We need Ohlen to answer that," said X'andria, gravely, "but I can tell you he isn't Ruprecht any more. Ohlen was blown back about twenty feet like he was a twig. Then what used to be Ruprecht stood up like nothing had even happened and just walked straight into all the goblins. And they didn't even attack him. It's like he's been turned into one of them."

"Ohlen, good god!" Gnome was struck with sudden realization. "We have to do something for him. Arden, can you help? X'andria, do you have anything?"

"I can get the arrow out." X'andria sighed heavily and focused on Ohlen's deflated form, his once-white robes dark and stained stiff with blood and dirt. "Arden, if I do, can you handle the wound?"

With Arden shifting across the cold dark earth into position, X'andria's left hand shot nimbly inside her robe and reemerged with fine silvery powder pinched between her forefinger and thumb. Firmly driving the butt of her torch into the ground, she moved to

Ohlen and positioned her small fingers and the powder just above the shaft and flights of the arrow protruding from inside his clavicle. Only now, as she hovered over Ohlen and the object cruelly piercing him, did she become aware of his rapid and shallow breaths. Breaths that seemed somehow weak and childlike, not at all the character of who she knew Ohlen to be.

X'andria allowed a miniscule amount of the powder to slip precisely from her fingers onto the shaft, marking it as the object of her intention. Still pinching the powder, her hand slowly descended just enough so as to grasp the very end of the arrow between her pinky and ring finger. As soon as she made contact she softly hissed the word. *Txaighirein*. Small. Her body shuddered as magic seeped from her, trailing heavily and quickly down her arm to mix with the powder and feast on the arrow in her grasp.

Arden heard the hiss, saw her slight frame convulse, and saw the powder in her fingers liquefy and rush to the arrow's shaft. A moment later dark blood began welling and oozing around the point where the arrow had entered Ohlen's body, between his neck and shoulder. Arden worried X'andria had somehow miscalculated. But then, eyes widening, he realized that the arrow was shrinking. Her gentle but firm grasp on the flight, was causing the arrow to retreat into her hand, rapidly becoming a miniature version of itself, in this way exiting Ohlen's wracked body without causing any more damage than already wrought.

All this happened in less than ten seconds. X'andria casually flicked the matchstick arrow into the pool and got out of the way so that Arden could dress the wound.

"Do you hear something?" Gnome's body was upright and rigid, eyes and ears focused intently back up into the darkness through which they had descended.

Chapter Nineteen

The stranger's moaning was almost intelligible now, and far too loud for their liking.

X'andria did not so much hear anything as she felt faint echoes in the earth of an approaching hoard. Gnome's senses were truly astonishing. She went swiftly to the stranger's massive form and placed her hand on one of the few parts that looked like it wouldn't cause pain, hoping a touch might comfort and silence him.

Finished now with his dressing, Arden placed himself, weapons at the ready, between Ohlen's prone body and anything that might come toward them from above. "Gnome," he breathed, "I'll need more light to be effective down here."

Kneeling, her hand on the stranger's slowly rising and falling stomach, X'andria's eyebrows came together as she gazed at the stone wall across the pool.

Is that what I think it is?

She could feel the tension behind her, she could sense the distant but impending doom approaching them, but maybe, just maybe, she had found something. Her head cocked sideways as she traced the faint lines in the masonry.

Moments later, eyes fixed on the point, she dashed to the water's edge and moved swiftly in, icy fingers immediately gripping her feet and ankles and calves. *Halfway there.* She had not taken her eyes from the spot.

Her feet were sticking in the muddy earth beneath the shallow pool. She could hear goblins approaching now, and she could hear her own feet swishing in the water, the noise amplified against the stone. She could feel Gnome's confusion and outrage and fear behind her. *Nearly there! But it looks so different from here.* Her confidence was faltering now, because up close the wall was all lichen and slime and aged cracks, and no clean hairline seams.

THE WALL

Eyes on the spot, X'andria, you know you never looked away.

And at last she was at the wall. Submerged to her thighs, shivering violently, she placed her frozen fingers firmly against the spot.

There was the briefest hint of resistance—resistance more of time than of substance. And then, with a gentle airy *whoosh*, the stone slipped forward, spinning a huge slab of the wall around a perfect fulcrum and revealing a large square into the unknown beyond.

Their heavy breathing echoed in this place. They dripped on cold, smooth stone. No one dared say anything for a while.

Chapter Twenty
INSIDE

His mind awoke to the sensation of icy daggers needling his skin in a shower of painful pricks. He saw nothing. The sloshing and rustling and breathing around him made no sense at all. The first things that did make sense to his groggy, foggy brain were the powerful hands hauling him out of the ice, hands that felt like they may crush his tender flesh in their vise-like grips, the sudden jerky movements causing his torn body to feel as though it might come apart into pieces.

Then, mercifully, he was left still.

Chapter Twenty

The next thing he remembered was dim light filtering through his tightly sealed and crusted eyelids. He must have passed out again, and once more his brain tried in vain to make sense of his condition. The pain was extraordinary, like he was floating in a sea of razor sharp blades and salt water, the hazy light promising a better world above if only he could get to the surface. Now there were whispers and shuffling. He heard a woman's voice.

He tried to ask a question.

There was agitation. Fear. Boudreaux could sense fear a mile away and he felt its rigid prickly pervasive presence now, heard it in the words he was just beginning to understand.

Then came her touch. Light, warm, perfect. It was the first thing that didn't hurt. It was the first thing that had felt good in a long time. With her touch came lucid consciousness, and his memory of all that had happened came rushing back. With clarity also came a wholly new and acute awareness of just how much damage he had sustained. *I must be in really bad shape.* But he could feel control of his body returning.

His eyelids resisted opening. He concentrated on each one in turn. *I have to break the surface, I have to see her.* With considerable effort, they finally cracked through the dried blood covering them. Matted eyelashes were surely torn off in the process, but that was the least of his concerns.

And then he saw her. She was blurry. She was blurry but she was beautiful, and she was staring at a point in the distance.

No sooner did he open his eyes, then she stood abruptly and dashed away like lightning. Turning his neck to follow her with his bleary eyes was more than he was prepared to attempt. He settled instead for the sound of sloshing water, and imagined what might be happening.

"Guys!" exclaimed X'andria in a barely contained whisper, "c'mon!"

Gnome and Arden turned and, eyes huge, immediately registered the enormity of what X'andria had discovered. As though they had practiced it a thousand times, Arden went immediately to Ohlen, scooped up his limp body, and bounded for the pool. Gnome grabbed X'andria's bag and dove headlong in as well. He was nearly at the wall, unable to touch ground with his toes, when he registered that he had passed X'andria going the wrong way.

"X'an," Gnome burbled, "no time!"

Arden unceremoniously hurled Ohlen through the door and then hoisted himself out of the water and through the opening.

"They're on us, X'an!" With only his head bobbing above water, Gnome's hand was outstretched for Arden to grasp, but his neck was craned to see behind him. "Leave him, X'an, there's nothing we can do!"

Their hands met, and Gnome was lifted from the icy liquid.

"Run, X'an! They're here. My god, X'an, I hear them!" Shouting now, "Run!"

X'andria heard them too. She heard them prowling and scuffling and snorting and shouting. But the stranger was *looking* at her. His eyes were open. She thought she could even sense a smile trying to break through the crusty mask of his face.

"I need you to move to that door," she whispered to him intently, "I need you to move now." More pleading and shouting from the door. "If you don't move right now, really fast, then we are both going to die."

Those were the magic words. Boudreaux's adrenaline fired, his body tensed, and he willed himself to action. As soon as she saw him flinch, X'andria dashed to the water, Boudreaux scrambling and lumbering close behind. Between another shot of cold water, the self-propelled motion, and screaming nerves, Boudreaux's head cleared enough to at least see the water, to see the door, and to understand the object of their flight.

Swishing to the wall behind her, Boudreaux saw X'andria hoist herself lithely out of the water and into the stone opening, before tumbling inside himself. The perfect door whooshed quietly closed behind them, sealing in total blackness, and sealing out death at the hands of the horrid piggy fiends.

Their heavy breathing echoed in this place. They dripped on cold, smooth stone. No one dared say anything for a while.

There was absolutely no sound coming from the other side of the secret door. The goblins must have arrived by now. They must have found X'andria's torch, their slimy snouts must have picked up the foreign scents. With any luck, the door's existence was a secret the goblins had never discovered, and would not discover any time soon.

"I'm Gnome," said Gnome brusquely. "You already met X'andria, and this here is Arden. Ohlen's out cold right now, kinda like you were until a minute ago."

"Boudreaux," rasped Boudreaux. It felt almost like he'd forgotten how to use his voice.

"What?" demanded Gnome.

"Boudreaux," he repeated, the voice a little steadier. "Don't know how you did, but thank you for saving me."

There was a pause. Then Arden whispered, "No one's saved just yet, Budo."

Their eyes were adjusting. Their ears were adjusting, too. Now that it appeared the imminent danger of goblin attack had faded, and the introductions were made, they heard the faint singing in the distance.

His head quickly disappeared beneath the surface of the water with only the faintest of ripples shuddering across the barely-lit surface.

Chapter Twenty-One
WONDERS AND HORRORS

They were in a square stone chamber. It was very dark, but not totally black because there seemed to be the faintest blue glow coming from an open archway on the far side of the room.

"What the hell...?" wondered Gnome aloud.

"Where are we?" asked Arden.

X'andria advanced slowly across the room, mesmerized by the soft glow and by the even softer sound.

"I'm gonna say dwarves," said Gnome, the slightest hint of disdain in his voice. "This wasn't put here by those pigs out there— they don't have any idea it's here—and the only beings I know who carve unnatural, square-edged, monstrosities like this underneath mother earth's perfect skirts," pausing for emphasis, "are dwarves."

Arden had never seen a dwarf. He'd heard about them, of

course, and heard the stories of gold and riches in palaces deep beneath the earth. Arden was an above-ground kind of person, though. He preferred birds and trees and clouds and skies and even rain, to dark and dirt and cramped small spaces with tons of rock and soil packed overhead waiting to fall on you and suffocate you.

X'andria could never have imagined anything like it. Turning the corner into the adjacent room, she was greeted with a whole universe of teeny winking lights covering the walls and descending down below the level of the floor into a small pool. She stared transfixed. Some kind of bioluminescent algae extended from the still clear water, stretched along the walls and just kissed the ceiling.

And it's singing!

Indeed the faintest purr filled the room. A gentle, reassuring hum caressed her ears, enticed her forward.

She took a step inside.

The small person was not very friendly. Boudreaux couldn't tell about the larger one yet. But they seemed pretty engaged in a discussion about dwarves and the relative merits of being above ground or below. Boudreaux reflected that he'd be happy in either place so long as he could have the intriguing girl with him, and so he took this opportunity to creep gingerly after her.

Many of his wounds had opened anew in the dash across the water. He was incredibly weak and nauseous, and rather unsteady— all ways Boudreaux was not used to feeling. But even so, he managed to get across the dark room without incident.

"Was *your* mom an elf, too?" Boudreaux croaked, hovering

stiffly in the archway. X'andria was startled to realize she had almost placed a foot in the water, she had been so totally entranced.

"Isn't it amazing?" she countered, turning, and trying to conceal the fact that she had completely lost control of her will. Approaching now, "How are you feeling, Budo? They almost killed you."

"Boudreaux," he winced. "My name is Boudreaux."

"Oh! Boudreaux! Sorry... I'm X'andria," she held out her hand. "Do you want something to eat? You must be starving."

Taking her hand gently, and feigning interest, "What is this place, X'andria?"

"I know, right? It's amazing! I've never seen anything like it. And if you listen carefully, you can hear the singing." X'andria skillfully extracted her hand from his lingering grasp.

The listening was interrupted before it began, however. "Whoa, what have we here?" Arden said as he and Gnome peered in from behind them.

Boudreaux advanced purposefully now toward the pool, it reminded him of something wondrous he'd seen long ago. "I wouldn't do that if I were you, Budo," Gnome warned in his best cautionary tone. "Looks and sounds underground can be really, really deceiving."

But it was too late.

Boudreaux dropped in. His head quickly disappeared beneath the surface of the water with only the faintest of ripples shuddering across the barely-lit surface.

The many thousands of tiny lights all went out. The singing stopped. It was pitch black. Arden, Gnome, and X'andria stood suspended in stunned silence.

His eyes were closed. The cool water felt like a million little hands swimming all around him, in and out and around all his hills and valleys, running gently along the ridges of his many wounds. They pulled him under with a gentle but firm tug, and just as quickly pushed him back to the surface. It felt bracing, it felt healing, and Boudreaux began to feel again the familiar power in his body.

"Ahhhhhh, this feels fantastic!" Boudreaux surfaced ebulliently, squirting water out of his mouth, and pushed his thick wet hair back out of his eyes. "I don't know what this is, but it's working wonders for me. You know what you need to do," he turned to the pool's edge, crossed his enormous arms on the edge, and fixed X'andria and her companions with his most dazzling smile: "You need to bring your passed-out friend in here for a swim. I feel fabulous, and I bet it will do him some good, too!" He added, "It doesn't seem like he could get much worse."

Gnome was resistant to this idea for all the right reasons, but as they discussed it, and time passed wherein Boudreaux did not drown, or start sweating profusely, or vomiting uncontrollably, or show other signs of major malady, they decided to try dipping Ohlen in the pool, too.

Evil. He was not evil, but he was surrounded by it. Or was he? Was it in him? Flayed bodies impaled on huge spikes swayed above the huddled masses, pathetic and fearful. He felt their fear and fed on it like sweet black nectar, thick with life's essence. The sky was red, his growing force of miserable slaves were patrolled and menaced from above, from below, from within. This was order and chaos together, and it was all his.

Ohlen's mind reeled from the vision. The deep darkness and sheer cruelty tore savagely into his spirit and left caustic residue throughout his body. His spirit was powerful, but he had never experienced anything remotely like this, and it had overwhelmed him. But now somehow, miraculously, he was being cleansed.

He felt a particularly virulent vein of deathly black in his chest. Even that, though, was being blessedly eroded, diluting and floating out and away from him like disease-ridden rats being washed from the hull of a ship by the sea.

And he remembered the arrow. He remembered the goblins. And with shocked realization, he remembered Ruprecht, the accursed marble, and those frightful piercing eyes.

Ohlen was under a long time. Boudreaux was just starting to think he should dive down to try and fetch him, when the tiny lights returned, the song resumed, and Ohlen burst out of the water at once gulping air and hysterically sobbing.

Looks like I'm headed to the forward station, too.

Chapter Twenty-Two
HELGA

She felt so ashamed as she watched the strange and powerful man turn and race away. His monstrous form, blurry through her tears, retreated back down the dark tunnel and disappeared from view. She wondered if she would ever see him again. She wondered if she would survive the hour.

She could not believe she had let it happen. The one thing he had specifically told her was to make sure no one got out and ran ahead. And she had failed. *That crazy old man.* One moment he had seemed asleep, the next he'd jumped up like he'd been shocked and had raced out of the dungeon. He had not even been interested in something to eat or drink. Clearly he had lost his mind, and Helga hadn't been able to stop him.

She was not accustomed to failure.

Chapter Twenty-Two

Helga was her parents' only daughter. Her mom was a baker and her dad a hunter. Between them they had supplied a significant amount of the bread and meat consumed by the people of Westover. From a very young age she learned to mix the ingredients for her mom's dark, heavy bread. Soon she knew her way around the hearth, and they taught her to select and grind the raw ingredients. Grinding was her least favorite part.

On her sixth birthday, her dad presented her with her first bow. It was a small bow, with short arrows of his own design. She had her first archery lesson with him that morning, and from that moment forth, no day passed without Helga venturing outdoors to test her mind, eyes, arms, and hands against the mysteries of the wind and the natural world.

The day her parents were murdered, she and her father had gone hunting. They went earlier than usual because of the terrors plaguing Westover at night. Lately, the animals seemed to have been sucked from the forest, and they came home empty handed, stomachs growling in anticipation of another light dinner.

Helga's family heard the cretins coming. They heard the savage attacks in nearby homes. They huddled together near the hearth, her mom with a large kitchen knife, both she and her dad with their bows and as many arrows as they could grab between them in the crazed terrifying moments before they'd been besieged.

When the monsters came, they did not use the door. That was unexpected. They tumbled in through windows, and somehow mounted the roof and pulled apart the thatch to fall in from above. Hell and merciless fury rained down on her family that night. Every one of her arrows found a mark. She felled many of the beasts. Her poor mother was the first to perish, knife in hand, screaming and wildly slicing. She and her dad methodically emptied their entire store of arrows into the oncoming rush of gnashing, menacing, drooling scoundrels.

Then they were out of ammunition—and though many dead and dying beasts littered their beleaguered home, still more came. Her father's attempts to protect her by hand combat were short lived, and his death was painful for her to recall, as was most of what had happened since.

That night was the first time she tasted failure, the first she felt tragic loss and deep sorrow. She had said only a few words since that night, but she had spent a great deal of time thinking, and she vowed to herself, if given an opportunity, she would do everything in her power to avoid ever feeling that way again.

And with that in mind, Helga clenched her small hands into little rock-hard fists, and blinked away the tears in her eyes. It was time to take a stand.

All the edible food was cleared from the storeroom. The first grotesque wall of pig man bodies was built and when she passed it she saw the scrawny boy she had been first imprisoned with cowering behind it, clutching a small sword he seemed barely able to lift.

Heaven, help us.

"What's your name?" she asked, her voice less gentle than she expected.

"Joseph," he answered timidly, eyes cast down.

"Stand up, Joseph," she commanded. "You must always be standing, always ready. You need to be looking around this wall so that you know who and what is coming toward you long before they are upon you. Do you understand?"

Joseph nodded, and stood immediately. Helga's forthrightness bled from her spirit, raced through the air, and infected him with purpose. "I will send more help soon. This is our forward post, and it must be the strongest."

Helga had a similar conversation with those stationed behind the second wall, before stalking back to the dungeon. *Now for the hard part.*

"Most of you are from Westover. You may not know me, but you have all eaten my mother Anna's breads, and been nourished by my father Robert's venison, boar and fowl." She had their attention. It smelled so horrid she thought she might retch, but she continued boldly, "This is our only chance. A great hero has freed us, has found us food, and has even found us some weapons. He has gone to protect the crazy man who ran. We can only hope that they will return alive. But we cannot wait, we must arm and organize ourselves, or we will perish in this filth."

Slowly they emerged from the dungeon. Helga's original band of distributors gave food and drink to the bedraggled and disoriented prisoners, while Helga set about the grisly task of digging through the remaining pile of bodies left by the stranger in search of any more usable weapons or armor.

She found several swords and daggers, two shields and a helmet. The two most enthusiastic of the new recruits, a brother and sister, received shields and swords and were sent to join Joseph at the forward station.

HELGA

But there was something else Helga uncovered, something that actually caused her to smile for the first time since before the attacks started in Westover. Slung on the shoulder of one of the cold corpses was a crude but serviceable short bow, and worn on its waist was a quiver of about a dozen arrows.

She placed the helmet firmly on her own head.

Looks like I'm headed to the forward station, too.

The pads of his feet rolled along the soil
like his bones were made of jelly.

Chapter Twenty-Three
TIME TO GO

They pulled the wet and dripping Ohlen, shivering with cold and shuddering with panic, from the strange pool. X'andria used the ends of his robes to dry him, before they helped him back into his clothes.

Boudreaux extracted himself from the water and jumped up and down to knock off the excess liquid from his glistening body, before vigorously shaking his head like a dog drying its fur.

"Hey, watch it, man!" Gnome and Arden were within spraying distance, and Gnome particularly disliked getting wet.

It seemed inappropriate to pepper Ohlen too quickly with the many questions they had for him, but it was also very hard to resist their curiosity. *How are you feeling? What happened to you? What happened to Ruprecht?*

Ohlen sat silently for several long minutes, nibbling on a few hard crackers that Arden had given him. As he gathered himself, Gnome and X'andria described all that had happened since he'd lost consciousness. They talked about Ruprecht's oddly mechanical gait as he walked into the wave of oncoming goblins, they introduced him to Boudreaux, X'andria described the discovery of the concealed doorway into what Gnome believed to be some kind of dwarf edifice, and they gestured at the mysterious pool that appeared to have healed Boudreaux's wounds and brought Ohlen back from the brink.

Finally, Ohlen spoke.

"This evil is new to me." He swallowed and took a sharp breath. "I've seen something, but I don't know what is real or what I've imagined. I can only hope that much of what I experienced was some figment brought about by my damaged body and spirit." Stronger now, "But this much I believe: our dear brother Ruprecht has been taken over by some monstrous being that is controlling him through that cursed black marble I somehow stupidly, carelessly let slip from my grasp." Ignoring X'andria's protestations about the arrow and that it was *not your fault*, he continued: "The goblins are the least of our concerns. They are just minions. Evil beings are drawn inexorably to more powerful evil. And what we're dealing with, my friends, is a vastly more powerful evil."

Boudreaux was not a particularly handsome man. He was phenomenally muscular, but now that the blood was cleaned from his face and hair, his rugged and angular features and toothy smile revealed a likeable but somewhat simple visage.

He noisily reaffixed the ridiculously small breastplate on his front and announced gruffly to the group, "I have three things to say. The first is that, when I arrived in this filthy hole, one of the tunnels led me past an opening into another part of this stone thing we're in. It's big, and there's a really scary statue. The second is that there are prisoners here, including one little girl named Helga. I promised I would help get her out alive. The third is that I'm leaving, right now, to make good on that promise, because god only knows what is happening to her and the rest of them right this minute."

To his own surprise, Gnome decided in that instant that he really, really liked Boudreaux.

When Arden stated they were coming with him, and that the whole reason they had entered this hellish place was to free those very same prisoners, Boudreaux seemed pleased. The fog of fear and doubt even lifted from Ohlen's mind with this renewed purpose, and soon they had gathered their few belongings, drawn their weapons, and pushed quietly back out through X'andria's secret door.

The tunnel was deserted. At least nothing was alive. Two devastated goblin corpses were mangled and twisted by the water's edge, having been savagely disemboweled by claws and teeth.

"The goblins do that to each other when they have disagreements," Gnome whispered knowledgeably to his new friend Boudreaux.

"You call them *goblins*?" Boudreaux queried. At Gnome's grim nod, he added, "A good name for them."

They were about halfway up the tunnel, still no signs of life, when Boudreaux continued thoughtfully, "Because you know how sometimes words kinda sound like what they are?" Trailing off now and pronouncing his new word slowly, deliberately, "*Goblins...*"

Arden's hand went up. The party tensed. They were near the main junction.

Chapter Twenty-Three

The vast space had just two goblins, rooting around and muttering to one another, in one of the depressions. Dagger between his teeth, Gnome lightly touched the back of Arden's right elbow, and dashed past him like a shadow along the wall. Boudreaux made to move as well, but Arden caught him while bringing the pointer finger of his free arm swiftly to his lips.

Quiet and quick, Gnome. The pads of his feet rolled along the soil like his bones were made of jelly. Underground, Gnome sensed terrain. In spite of himself, he had come to like the world above, but it felt so good to be back, moving with the waves within the earth.

The goblin nearest him inclined its head slightly. *It smells me. It's first, then.* Gnome saw the moves before him: left, right, left, leap to bank, right off bank, fly, attack. Goblin One was upright sniffing one moment, and lay gurgling on the ground the next, eyes rolling back in its nearly severed head. The second was aware that its companion had fallen, but had not even seen the assailant. *I am shadow*, Gnome recalled the mantra of his mentor. Seconds later, Goblin Two joined its brother gasping and twitching in the earth, blood welling from a deep dagger wound just below the base of its skull.

They had heard the quiet assault across the chamber, but were surprised moments later when Gnome slid wordlessly back into formation behind Arden, eyes fixed ahead.

"Where, Boudreaux?" breathed Arden.

"Back to the blood bath, straight through the far side, third right."

The combat zone was grisly and smelly. No effort whatsoever had been made to clean it up. Things moved in the room, but they were the foul little things that death attracts, the bloodworms and beetles, the flies and the rats.

TIME TO GO

Entering the open space, Arden's pace hastened considerably. Moving in concealment would not be possible, so best just to be quick about it. In order to run, Boudreaux had to grasp the goblin-sized breastplate in both hands and hold it slightly away from him. Stark naked as he was otherwise, this made for an incredibly humorous sight for Ohlen, X'andria, and Gnome, who were positioned behind him. Even surrounded as they were by gory horror, X'andria and Gnome both found it difficult not to laugh. The return to this space, however, sent Ohlen's thoughts spiraling far away into the recesses of his mental reserves, where laughter was not a resident.

Miraculously they crossed the battlefield unmolested. Real or imagined, X'andria's sharp ears registered some small sound behind them, but their plan called for forward trajectory to the prisoners at all costs, and they dashed onward into darkened tunnels familiar only to the newest member of their party.

Boudreaux dashed ahead unchallenged by Arden. *I'm coming Helga, hold on.* They were running full out now. Boudreaux was a good ten feet in front when he dashed right and out of sight down the third tunnel.

On they flew. Suddenly they came upon bodies. Eight or nine goblins lay strewn about the tunnel on their faces, on their backs and on their sides, with arrows sprouting from their foreheads, eyes and throats.

Further on, the party caught up to find Boudreaux crouched over a toppled stack of goblin corpses. He was rooting around inside it and had extracted the bloody bodies of a teenage boy and girl, a small rusty sword falling from the girl's limp grasp. Boudreaux's forward post had been breached.

They tore on.

Boudreaux stopped abruptly and the others plowed into him

from behind. The second wall still stood.

"Helga!" he shouted. Gnome did not like the shouting at all, but now didn't seem to be the time for a lesson in tactics for their newest recruit.

"Helga, it's me—Boudreaux!"

And there she was. Helga stepped slowly from behind the wall of goblins. She had a bow with one notched arrow held in her left hand, her skinny legs planted defiantly in a wide and stable archer's stance. Her arms were dirty and blood-smeared and her small round face furrowed with a worry and anguish rarely seen in anyone so young.

But she was alive! Boudreaux ran toward her, and in that moment, the grim archer transformed back into a young girl. Her troubled features blossomed into a proud grin, and her huge blue eyes opened wide in realization that the impossible had come to be. The bow fell from her hand, clattering to the earth, and she ran to meet him.

On his knees now, Boudreaux received her embrace, her tiny body folding into his massive frame. *This is what matters*, Boudreaux decided. *This is all that matters.*

"Let's get you home," he managed through big, heavy tears.

His grasshopper exploded into a hundred demonic fiery serpents that rose straight into the air and then flew directly at the eyes of the waiting goblins.

Chapter Twenty-Four
MOVING OUT

"Okay everyone, here's how it's going to work." Gnome, ever the strategist, had taken charge of the Westoverans while Boudreaux, Arden, and Ohlen guarded the still-standing defensive post.

"We need to line up three across—X'an, can you help?" There were eighteen remaining, which meant a line six long, and three deep. Joseph, the sheepish boy who was the smallest of them all, was placed in the middle of the group.

Once they were arranged, Gnome continued, "We're giving our six shields to those on the left side. With good luck, we'll walk right out with no need to use them. But lately, this place hasn't exactly been handing out the good luck. So," Gnome paused for effect, "if the bad guys come at us, the first thing that happens is everyone gets close together this way." He motioned squishing them together with his arms. "Let me see you do that now."

This did not go smoothly at first, because most of them could not actually see Gnome very well, if at all. Eventually, with X'andria stepping in to help explain, the thin, bedraggled group squished together quite effectively.

X'andria stayed by Gnome's side to mime the actions, "Next, you need to crush back gently but firmly to the nearest wall behind you, while those on the outside raise your shields to form a wall of protection."

It was not a very good-looking wall. The shields were too small, were held at odd angles, and there were many areas of exposure. But after practicing the maneuver four times, with pointers here and there from Gnome and X'andria, Gnome was satisfied that it was as good as it was going to get, and most certainly better than nothing.

"We know the way out of here. And the route we are taking will always have those of you on the right walking next to a wall. So if you can stay in this formation, you will always be able to retreat into your protective wall at any time. If any danger comes, do not break formation, do not run, do not try to fight. Please leave that to us. If I yell *wall*, you'll know what to do. Does everyone understand?"

Glum silence.

"Okay then. Boudreaux, Arden, and X'andria, take the lead; Westoverans in the middle; Ohlen and I in the rear. Let's move out."

And so they did. It was not a quiet procession, but it was orderly. They left the tunnel leading to the dungeon, turned left, and approached the scene of the earlier battle.

Ice rolled over Ohlen's skin, and permeated the flesh around his lungs. "Something is coming," he breathed to Gnome.

On they marched.

The hall was a grisly scene. X'andria immediately wished they had said something to the prisoners to prepare them for what they were going to see. Goblin bodies were sprawled on top of one another, rats lapped at dark congealed pools of blood, it smelled awful, and part way across the space lay the twisted remains of the crazy old prisoner who had run out.

Still the march went on. To their credit, no one wavered. There was not even an audible breath or a whisper. This group had seen more than their fair share of horror, and they marched forward in stoic silence behind the leaders.

Halfway through the room, it happened. They were exposed on three sides, and too far in to retreat back to the safety of the tunnel, when goblins streamed into the space and filled the mouths of both tunnels they had yet to explore, as well as the exit they were intending to take toward the surface. A party of a dozen or so even raced around the perimeter of the carnage to block their retreat—a different tactic altogether. While there was much slobbering and gnashing of teeth, there was also a very thinly held restraint keeping the beasts from engaging. The Westoverans were being carefully surrounded for a massacre.

"Wall." Gnome commanded firmly. The villagers acted quickly and quite effectively, crushing their thin bodies together, and cowering behind their puny shields.

At that moment, the reason for the goblin's tactical order became obvious. Gliding into the chamber from the right hand tunnel, was a tall man-sized being in black robes, just like the one they had seen in the forest. Ohlen shivered, and began to meditate.

Gnome thought quickly. Extracting his second and final grasshopper from his tunic, he raced forward to Arden. "I'll lead them out," he growled. "You kill everything."

Chapter Twenty-Four

The hiss that then sprayed from Gnome's mouth was pure venom. *Svres'kha'belduurawf.* Fear. His grasshopper exploded into a hundred demonic fiery serpents that rose straight into the air and then flew directly at the eyes of the waiting goblins. In truth there was no fire, and there were no serpents, but Gnome had a particular gift for making people believe what he wanted them to see, especially those with relatively dim wit.

He outdid himself with this one. Panicked goblins fled in all directions.

"Westoverans, follow me," he roared, and as soon as they heard him, he dashed toward the exit, toward the main junction, toward the rising tunnel on the far side, and toward the outside world.

Boudreaux escorted the fleeing party to the room's edge. He wanted to see Helga safely from the room, and as she flashed out of sight, they exchanged the briefest of glances—fear and determination reflecting in those big blue eyes.

Though Gnome's illusion had been effective, many goblins remained who had not fallen for the trick, or who were recovering quickly. One fired two arrows in rapid succession at the fleeing prisoners. One missed wide, but the second likely would have found a mark had Boudreaux not leapt in front of it to take the shot with his absurd little breastplate.

Black oily ropes issued lightning fast from the fingertips of the robed figure, and flew across the space to pin Ohlen forcefully against the wall. These were the same bonds he'd seen Arden struggle beneath days before in the forest. Breathless from the blast, Ohlen struggled against the sticky writhing strands to no effect. Slithering tightly around him, he was soon almost completely cocooned with only part of his face and his left hand visible.

Arden had been standing right next to him when Ohlen was

snapped away with a powerful squelch. With Boudreaux engaged on the far side, this left only Arden and X'andria fighting the ten or so goblins remaining at the center of the battle.

Nine goblins now. One of X'andria's darts struck the snout of the nearest assailant, who spun around wailing and clutching his face.

Arden blurred into a raging windmill of steel. His blows were designed not to stick or to graze, but to sever and fully disable. And sever he did. In less than a minute, only half the goblins remained in their vicinity, these prowling at a safe distance.

Just then, the thing's hood slid back to reveal a deathly white hairless man with jet black eyes. More of the black ropes issued from him and they hit Arden with phenomenal force, blasting him back roughly onto the ground.

Time slowed for Boudreaux. He was in the middle of crushing two goblin skulls together when he saw Arden knocked out of operation by a second wave of wriggling black ropes. This left only X'andria, surrounded by five goblins, with the bald menace advancing toward her, too, like floating death incarnate.

Boudreaux took a painful dagger to the ribcage from one of several foe surrounding him, as his mind raced. *Not X'andria, you bastards.*

Gnome ran as fast as he dared, mindful that he could only move at the speed of the slowest in his flock. His trick had been incredibly effective, their way had been cleared, but he saw that passing dazed goblins were shaking off the vision and noticing the prisoners' flight.

Just keep running. We might lose a few, but to stop is to die.

Chapter Twenty-Four

On they ran. Through the main junction, into the first rising tunnel. Helga was right behind him.

"Helga," he panted, "go straight at the next fork, not left, straight—it will take you up and out. I will stay behind and guard the rear." No response. Gnome had to look behind himself to make sure she was still there. She was. She was running, breathing hard, and listening to his every word. "Helga, Westover is no more. Fly to Bridgeton. There you will find Rowena, and she will protect you. Do not stop, do not slow!"

And with that, Gnome stepped aside into the mouth of the left fork, and watched the gaggle of prisoners lope by, hope and terror in each and every face.

And then he heard the goblins. Too many of them. Gnome would be able to cause trouble. Gnome would be able to keep them from following the prisoners. But this was not a battle Gnome could win.

Gnome used the only natural advantage he had left: his small size. He snuck around the edge of the tunnel's fork like shadow mixing in darkness, and then sprang low and headlong, twisting his body rapidly, into the feet of the onrushing goblin pursuers. The leaders toppled over him, the followers piled on above, and those behind crushed into the rear. Gnome was pinned at the bottom of the grotesque pile.

Ohlen had one eye left unmasked by the snaking black fingers, through it he watched the robed figure closely as it bound Arden. It was calling forth its dark forces by incantation. "His mouth, X'andria!

He needs his voice!" But the instant Ohlen shouted his own animated bonds forced their way into his mouth brutally silencing and choking him.

X'andria's mind whirred.

Boudreaux, spurred on by the dagger in his rib cage, and his visceral fear for X'andria's well-being, dropped the sword he was holding and went into full-on grapple mode. *Two weapons are better than one*, he thought savagely, as he plowed into the nearest couple of goblins and flung them like big juicy toys to splat heavily against the wall nearby. Spinning as he pulled the dagger from between his ribs, he stole a glance in her direction.

What is she doing? Her darts, which he had noticed she threw very adroitly, and with deadly accuracy, were strewn on the ground around her like she had dropped them. She plunged a hand inside her robes and brought it back out like a flash, with some kind of dust blooming in a cloud around her head. Her face was a knitted web of concentration. That was all he was able to see, before he was reengaged with the relentless aggression surrounding him.

Mouth. Tongue. Voice. Fly. Destroy. Silence. These are the things she envisioned as she spat out the word. *Txaighirein.* Small. Words always carried some measure of pain, always felt like some part of her body was being exhaled violently through her mouth. But this was worse. She was aiming for an object far away, and the sensation was one of coughing up part of her lung in an effort to hit a small target some twenty-five feet away.

X'andria pitched forward off-balance. If she had had full control of her wits, this might have been convenient with the darts arrayed on the ground around her. But she was fighting for consciousness, and struggled to get her hands to obey as they groped shakily for her prized weapons. Shadows closed in around her.

Gnome took a mouthful of hot goblin blood as he stuck and twisted his knife into the now-squealing beast lying directly on top of him. Beside him, a standing goblin pitched over wailing as the main tendon in its left leg was mysteriously severed.

But two freebies were all he would get. They quickly figured out which of the bodies was not one of theirs, which was the one causing them to bleed, which was the one to be destroyed. It was a wild frenzy of claws and fists that rained upon him. His knife clattered to the ground as he tried helplessly to protect himself from the onslaught.

Loud and totally inhuman screeching billowed from the bald and morbidly pale man. He spun like a dervish clutching at his throat, and sank to the ground in a heap of flailing limbs.

X'andria looked up in time to see the five goblins around her— with their leader incapacitated and so many fallen brethren—fleeing madly in all directions. She noticed Boudreaux standing upright, his few remaining combatants also skittering away, his mouth agape as he stared between her and the screaming, roiling pile of black robes nearby.

Boudreaux quickly recovered and tore across the room to pounce bodily on the pale man, with an audible crunch. The screeching did not stop, but seemed to change in character with the impact. Boudreaux tore apart the man's robes like they were tissue paper, flopped him roughly onto his stomach and used the torn fabric to hog tie him tightly, with his arms straining backward to connect to his ankles, his body arched painfully backward.

With the man's incapacitation, the strength of the bonds holding Ohlen and Arden began to fail. Soon they were disentangling themselves, and stepping forward from the limp, slippery snakes. Ohlen was hacking and spitting oily black sludge from his aching mouth.

"I don't *ever* want to be stuck in those damn things again!" muttered Arden, to no one in particular, as he shook the last of the recalcitrant ropes from his right leg.

X'andria, Ohlen, and Arden approached Boudreaux in time to see him forcefully flip the sputtering man onto his side.

"Now *this* is something I think I could really use," Boudreaux was saying as he unbuckled and unlaced the man's gleaming plate torso and leg armor, previously obscured by his robes. In a few moments the man was almost completely nude, and Boudreaux was absorbed in bending and fitting the various pieces onto his own massive frame.

What lay before them, then, was a nude and alabaster white, extremely thin, struggling man with jet black eyes. Though there were no pupils, it was clear from the moment he was flipped onto his side that his full focus was on Ohlen. Pure hatred.

"What did you *do* to him, X'andria?" Arden asked, scanning suspiciously all around them as if expecting more unwanted visitors.

"I think I shrunk his tongue," she returned cheerfully. "At least that's what I meant to do!"

"He's got a black marble too, Ohlen," pointed out Arden.

They had all seen it. The shiny black marble was smack in the middle of his chest, like a third eye peering angrily out at them.

X'andria pointed, "And do you see that purple streak running up from his foot, through his leg, and through his belly? He must have first contacted it with his foot, and it must have swum through him, the way it did with Ruprecht. Poor guy."

A moment later she continued, "What do we do, Ohlen? He seems to really not like *you* at all."

"I don't know, exactly," Ohlen said slowly, thoughtfully, "I don't think I can touch him. That didn't go well at all last time. If I had time, maybe I could turn him, but the evil is so..." While searching for the right word, Ohlen registered rapid movement to his right and cried, "No Boudreaux!"

Boudreaux, decked out in his new armor, had retrieved two small double-edged goblin axes from among the dead. With feline quickness he knelt before the prone captive, holding the axes by the blades, and began digging as if using a clamshell, directly into the flesh around the marble with both blades.

If they thought they had heard screeching from the man before, this was a whole new level. Straining mightily against his bonds and sputtering and spewing, he protested vainly against Boudreaux's aggressive assault. For its part, the marble seemed to sense the attack and began swimming around in the man's flesh, for a moment even disappearing beneath the surface in a pool of red.

It only took a moment, though. Boudreaux's powerful and clearly directed blades sunk deep and quick beneath the marble and he came away with a wedge of flesh containing the marble within it.

The marble's many vicious barbed arms spun and churned through the small clump of meat, looking desperately for a host, and liquefying the flesh around it in the process. In about ten seconds, the flesh had melted away entirely and the marble ceased all motion, returning to an inanimate state balanced precariously between

Boudreaux's dripping clamshell axe blades.

"I'll take that, Boudreaux. Be very careful no one touches it," Ohlen's voice shook slightly as he produced his round ivory case beneath Boudreaux's blades, and sealed the marble within once more.

Working quickly, Arden used a combination of herbs from his pack, and pieces of the man's black robes to slow the bleeding from the enormous gaping wound left in his chest. X'andria stooped over his unconscious head and pried open an eyelid.

"Not creepy and black any more," she reported.

Gnome, cowering beneath a wave of brutality, recalled the disemboweled and partially eaten goblin corpses they had passed when exiting the dwarf lair.

God, this hurts, he thought, feeling exhausted and alone.

Ohlen's meditation deepened.

Chapter Twenty-Five
HERE, THERE, EVERYWHERE

"What should we do with him?" asked Arden, his skillful hands finishing the slimy work of packing the unconscious man's gaping chest wound.

Arden, X'andria, and Boudreaux all looked expectantly at Ohlen for an answer to this question, but none came: Ohlen seemed lost in thought.

Boudreaux suggested they get the man to the mysterious healing pool. "We need to get out of here anyway," he reasoned, "and that place seems pretty safe." Without Gnome to disagree, and with Ohlen in another world, they soon found themselves scuttling quickly from the scene of the battle, the unconscious man in Arden's arms.

Chapter Twenty-Five

Ohlen glided along contemplatively behind. *Light, love, beauty, humanity. I see it first in my mother's smile. Her warmth and love radiates to me. And I know it is the love of mothers everywhere. Purest good. Feel it. Extend out from this depth, reach high and bring that powerful and abundant blessing to this space. Fill up with light. And concentrate now, where is your center? Where is that golden glow of goodness spinning and thriving? My joints tingle with power. My chest expands. But it's just beneath my heart and lungs that the sphere is deepest, most dense and most vibrant.*

The beating Gnome was taking could not be survived much longer. *If I stay, I will die,* he thought, as he rolled side to side, doing his best to shield himself with his arms. In order for them to get in their brutal turns hitting and clawing, the body on top of him had been dragged away. So there was nothing left pressing directly down on him, and that meant he might actually be able to move.

Gnome drew a burst of energy from the last of his reserves. Rolling sharply to his left he made it onto his stomach and crawled furiously through the dirt between the first set of legs he saw. He was small, but not so small as to sail cleanly through the squat goblin legs. Instead he lodged between them, the howling cluster of savages clawing at the slick black leather covering his calves to drag him back into the open for more punishment.

He knew this was his last chance. He kicked at the claws behind him and scrabbled forward between the straddling legs. He shrunk to his smallest, thinnest self, and tried to squirt through. From the sounds and the shoves above him, he knew he was at least partly successful. He heard shouts and snarls of frustration and felt pressure and awkward shifting all around him as he squeezed forward.

Meanwhile, Ohlen's meditation deepened. *I smile. The sun shines on my face even in darkness. Good will persists through treachery. Good deeds beget good deeds. The sun warms my skin even through my clothes. I feel it long after night has fallen. For I am the sun. With smiles, good will, good deeds, and warmth, we bring sunshine to our lives, and we hasten its return to the heavens each morning.*

And at that moment, another mind was raging.

They dare defy me? Me! The pathetic worms have no idea of the torment I prepare for them. How dare they! I will cut them, and it will be slow. Terribly slow. There is no end to the pain I prepare for them. They took one of my eyes! I will take both of theirs in return. I will take everything they hold dear. I will destroy everything they know.

Gnome was through the squat straddling legs! He stayed low. He stayed in shadow. Moving as quickly as possible, he raced between his tormentors. They clubbed and clawed and sliced and bit as he wove between them, but as often as not their startled attacks at his narrow darting form found purchase on their neighbors instead of him. The resulting confusion and cacophony was tremendous.

They were hot on his heels. He was limping badly, he was

bleeding, he was weaponless. Even so, his preternatural speed, fueled by a level of adrenaline accessible only when literally running for one's own life, led him to outpace the shoving grunting beasts, and by a good measure. He was heading down the very first right-hand path they had taken, and he paused just long enough to shove open the iron door to the holding cell that they had first inspected what seemed a lifetime ago. *That will give them a puzzle to work out* he thought, as he tore further on, into uncharted territory.

The party had reached the tunnel to the pool and the secret door. It seemed they were not followed. Walking through the large cavernous junction caused X'andria to wonder aloud, "What about Gnome?" Arden was quick to reply, "Gnome knows what he's doing. If anyone will be okay down here, it's Gnome."

They descended the chilly tunnel in silence. Halfway down, Boudreaux offered to help Arden carry the unconscious man, and Arden gratefully accepted. Waist-deep in the icy pool at the base of the tunnel, X'andria pushed silently through the perfectly concealed door – no one else could see where it was. They piled into their mysterious sanctuary.

Ohlen's inspiration deepened.

My companions embody greatness. I share in their essence, and they in mine. Open to them. Overcome your corporeal singularity and bathe in the powerful spirits around you. Expand with their might, their conviction, their selfless courage.

I am a vessel to concentrate the goodness in this world, manifest in love for our children, in generosity, in sunshine, in X'andria and

Arden, and Gnome and in Boudreaux. Absorb and embody omnipotent benevolence so that I may rise to this present challenge. I, Ohlen, am in everything, and everything is in me.

And, close by, the rage hit a boiling point.

Why are they so weak? So stupid? I feed them, herd them, lead them, teach them. I threaten them, torment them, flay them, and burn them. Yet still they fail. They always fail. They frighten, they run, they hide. Such weakness. I have waited so long. Soon I will be everywhere, I will own everything, and I will destroy them and all their offspring. I will breed more of them just so I can exterminate them all over again.

Gnome had lost the goblins. He could no longer hear them in pursuit. He could hardly believe he was alive, but now was no time to celebrate. Now was a time for caution. His chief aim was to find his friends before losing any more strength. He crept onward.

Suddenly the tunnel split open on the right side. The gap revealed a huge, well-lit stone room, and he recognized instantly the handiwork of dwarves. Hugging the shadows as he was, he couldn't see into the room, but he could tell there was activity, he could hear there were sentient beings, and he knew he did not want to meet them.

Opposite the opening, there was no shadow to hide in. But turning back was not an option, waiting was not an option, and the gap was not very big. So he decided simply to dash across and hope that, if someone saw him, it would be brief and blurry enough as to not attract attention.

So dash he did. He dashed as only Gnome could dash.

Chapter Twenty-Five

But he was seen. He was seen by a pair of petrifying eyes. Even though his movement across the gap took the briefest of instants, those huge, blazing eyes caught him and held him and examined him like they were looking straight through his skin and bones and into his very soul. What Gnome would puzzle over in his terrified and frantic flight onward, was that it seemed the eyes belonged to an inanimate statue.

Come to me, you sniveling cretins. You take what belongs to me? I will hold you down. I will pierce your flesh with burning embers. You will scream in agony. I will torment one, while the others watch. You will beg, you will cry, you will throw yourselves at my feet for mercy and you shall have none. You will have only pain. And I will laugh. Ruprecht will laugh in the face of your pathetic agony.

In moments, light sprang to life in her hands.

Chapter Twenty-Six
WATER AND LIGHT

The stone room was dark and cold, but it felt safe. The faint singing emanating from the adjacent room sounded soothing and welcoming.

"This is a good place," Ohlen murmured, his first words in some time.

Boudreaux wasted no time carrying the badly wounded man to the pool. He set him gently down at the edge of the water, and slid him smoothly into the dark liquid. As before, blue lights danced and winked, reflecting playfully in the ripples on the pool's surface. Boudreaux could actually feel the water gently tugging on the man from the moment his feet were inserted, like it wanted him to enter, wanted to heal his broken body. And, as before, as soon as Boudreaux let go, the lights blinked out and the singing stopped, the man disappeared beneath, and all became silent and black as pitch.

Chapter Twenty-Six

"X'andria, do you have another torch?" asked Arden, "If we're going to stay here a while, I'd love some light."

X'andria rummaged dutifully in her small bag and felt her last travel torch. In moments, light sprang to life in her hands.

It was an elegant arched chamber with a domed stone ceiling formed by eight ornate curving wedges. The mysterious luminescent material was revealed to be a pale white mossy growth beginning beneath the surface of the shallow pool and climbing up the near wall to expand slightly outward, partially covering two segments of the ceiling.

But the room's illumination came with a mournful gasping scream. The instant the light hit the moss, it began wailing. The same barely audible chorus of voices they had heard previously, suddenly exuded agony, sadness and regret.

"Put it out, X'andria!" Ohlen cried. She was, of course, already hastily extinguishing the flame, while turning her body instinctively to shield the room, and the moss, from the light.

Darkness again. The only sound was their rapid breathing.

"What happened?" asked Arden urgently.

"The light was hurting it," X'andria moaned. "The room is covered in runes. I can't read them, but there must be a lot of power locked in here, and that amazing singing stuff is infused with it."

"It's gone now," said Ohlen in a careful monotone. "The spirit is no more."

"The guy!" Boudreaux exclaimed, and jumped into the water with a splash.

They heard some thrashing about as Boudreaux searched for the man's submerged body. A short while later, he surfaced again. "I've got him!" he cried, clambering out of the pool and dragging the unconscious waterlogged body behind. Then, much more subdued,

"You're right, Ohlen. The water is dead. It doesn't feel anything like it did before."

Arden and X'andria expelled a fair amount of breath apologizing and taking responsibility for killing the magical, healing moss. Ohlen reminded them patiently and repeatedly that none of them knew light would destroy the material, that it could have been any of them that did it, and that they should not feel guilty about it. Boudreaux sat quietly steeping in his own sour and sardonic thoughts that included *Perhaps if I drown all three of these idiots right now I'll have some peace and quiet.*

Boudreaux's hand roamed in the dark to the neck of the wet, clammy man to feel for breath and pulse. "Well, if the stuff's dead, why don't we at least get the light going again so we can see what the hell is going on?" he suggested gloomily, adding, "And this guy's still breathing. At least for now."

There were just the two rooms. The mossy growth was indeed shriveled and brown and flaking from the wall and ceiling by the time X'andria's light shone again. In spite of what had just happened, she found herself overcome and awestruck at the slanting script runes covering the walls and ceiling. It was as though they were parchment and the elegant writing had been penned effortlessly into the stone. She knew, though, that no hand had written these marks, that no chisel had carved these symbols. What surrounded her was elemental power made manifest in stone as words blasted into existence by magical thought.

Holding the torch on her tummy in both her small hands, she lay down on the floor and stared at the ceiling and the symbols like a child gazing up at constellations in the sky.

Ohlen knelt next to Boudreaux, and placed his hand tentatively on the naked man's forehead. Boudreaux had removed the black bandages to check the massive wound, and was surprised to find it had been partially healed. A paper thin layer of tender pink skin had closed around the bloody gaping hole left by his violent extraction of the black marble. Boudreaux placed the wet strips of cloth over the man's nethers more to improve his own view, than out of any concern for decency.

Ohlen felt strong now. Powerful waves of life-giving purpose radiated through his core. There was not the violence and rage and fathomless power in this man like the force that had blown Ohlen physically and spiritually away from Ruprecht. There were, however, traces of all those things in this man's soul and in his body, like the lingering smell of smoke in one's hair, days after the campfire has gone out.

The eyes followed Gnome as he raced down the dark, twisting passage. It was like trying to outrun a raging fire wildly burning the forest path behind you. Heat and death were in those eyes, loathing and intense hatred smoldered in pursuit.

But he ran. The temptation had been to give up. To give in to the powerful gaze. But he had not. He fought back the urge, and he limped along downward as fast as his weary, battered legs would take him.

He skidded out into the big battle room, now thick and heavy with festering death. His quick and skillful feet pounded through putrid sticky pools and over and around bloating bodies. He knew where to go and he knew speed was his only ally.

The closer he came to the secret door, the more his mind raced with fear. *Are they behind me? Have they heard me?* He plowed into the frigid stale water in the total darkness and swam, quickly in over his head, to the massive stone wall. *God I'm tired. Just a bit further.* Heart thumping in his throat and ears, Gnome reached and pushed on the slimy, scaly wall. *Where was it?* He could now hear his pursuers closing in behind him. His mind raced.

Treading water with one bad leg, and thoroughly exhausted, his nimble fingers searched rapidly for evidence of a seam he knew he would not find. *It's higher than I can reach!* Relaxing his body for a moment, he sank into the murky blackness, and then kicked violently to rise high out of the water. At his highest point he pounded the stone wall with his fist. *Open, damn you! I need you to open.* Nothing. Goblins were close now. Body and mind screaming and rebelling he tried again, and again and again.

Gnome began to cry.

This is how it ends. I led them out, at least. I fought. I ran. I helped my friends. And now I die. Cold, wet Gnome, all alone, and unable to reach the goddamn door.

And it was in that state, paddling slowly to stay afloat, and feebly fumbling at the unyielding cruel dwarfish stone, that light bloomed above him, and his friend Arden reached out and saved his life.

The mass of spiraling energy dove out of the ether and plowed directly down into her little body, which arched dramatically, glowed brightly, and lifted several feet off the ground.

Chapter Twenty-Seven
POWER AND PAIN

Power loomed above her—locked in the mystery of the many runes. *So many symbols.* Her head was swimming in the circles and lines. Their sheer awesome beauty was intoxicating, drawing her toward their majesty, as did all things ethereal. X'andria's inquisitive eyes lingered on something familiar. *Wait a minute. I know you.*

"It just popped into my head," Arden was explaining. He stripped off Gnome's freezing wet clothes and wrapped him in a cloak. Boudreaux had asked how in the world he had known to open the door for Gnome. "You guys were busy, and I was walking around in here wishing I hadn't asked X'andria to light that torch, when it just hit me. *Gnome probably can't get to the door.* So I peeked out, and there he was!"

The man's inert body was cold from the pool, and the chilly room, and the fact that he was naked apart from the damp shreds of robes Boudreaux had strategically placed over him. But his forehead, where Ohlen touched him, was burning hot.

Ohlen willed his consciousness into the man's troubled spirit-space.

Tremendous ability. Confidence and knowledge. The pathways of intellectual prowess were thoroughly paved. But it was all askew. Damaged. Ohlen hurtled at incredible speeds through a grand palace of a mind built for peak performance, but it was foggy, disconnected, totally confused. *Stop. I have to stop. This is too much!* With effort he achieved stillness, his spirit presence buffeted by torrential and manic winds. His solidity caused disruption around him. The consciousness he had invaded was reacting to his presence. Stationary now he was able to see more clearly. His light and warmth shone out into the windy stormy haze encircling him. Ohlen looked for signs of malice and fear like a hunter tracking its prey.

X'andria was lost in excitement. An entire segment of the ceiling was written in symbols she could read! Once she was looking at it properly, the words and meanings began to jump off the wall toward her like they existed in three-dimensional space. Stealing glances at the other sections, she now guessed that each of the eight was written in a different language. Before it had all just looked like ornate gibberish, but now her sharp mind began to parse the subtle differences between the character types. *Life*, she realized in wonder, *this room is a shrine to the essence of life.*

"What do you mean you killed it?" Gnome coughed out the words in disappointed indignation. "That stuff is the whole reason I came down here and nearly drowned in that disgusting water out there!" If Arden thought he felt bad before, this was a whole new level of guilt. Ignoring his morose mumbled apologies, Gnome continued, "How do you know it's dead? Maybe it's just sleeping or resting or something."

"It's totally dead, Gnome," Boudreaux cut in. "The magic singing stuff is brown and shriveled, falling off the wall, and the pool feels totally different, too. The creepy guy was in there when it happened and I had to fish him out. He was kind of... half done, I guess you could say."

"The creepy guy?" Outraged, Gnome looked incredulously between Boudreaux and Arden. "You brought **him** back here?"

Arden stared guiltily at the floor, Boudreaux found himself at a rare loss for words.

"And X'andria should have known better!" Gnome wailed, continuing on undeterred. "She's supposed to know all about stuff like this." Now yelling, "X'andria, come in here and explain yourself!" Gnome trailed off in another fit of sputtering coughs.

Hearing her name shouted nearby caused X'andria to snap out

of it. "Gnome!" she cried, and bounded over.

This is so thick. Moving his mind toward the darkest mass felt like pushing his brain through a sieve. *This must be where the marble was lodged.* He stopped. No more searching, no more pushing, no more moving. It was dangerous here. The forces around him were hungry and confused. It would be easy to get lost.

But that would be another day. Today Ohlen, strengthened by his meditations, was the one to be feared. And he turned his focus inward to himself. His core was shining and burning bright like molten ore. He coaxed it outward, invited the laughter and joy and love and devotion to pour out of him like rays of sunshine on a fresh spring morning streaking into a dark forgotten cave that had been newly discovered and opened wide for all to see.

Gnome was not in good shape. He was clearly upset. X'andria's bright smile faltered at seeing the fear in his eyes, his small body wrapped up like a baby on the floor, his left leg sticking out at a slightly odd angle.

"Oh Gnome!" she fell to the floor at his side and hugged him, "You're back! Everything is going to be okay, Gnome, you're going to be fine. What happened to you?"

Calmed by X'andria's genuine care and warm touch, Gnome recounted his tale. He explained about the race to the surface, about the goblins in pursuit, about sending Helga to Bridgeton and Rowena. He even got a bit animated when describing his headlong dive into the legs of the pursuing goblins, the fight that ensued, and his flight from their clutches.

When Gnome got to the part about the statue and the terrible eyes, Boudreaux interjected, "That's exactly what I saw!" The two of them fell to recounting the details of their dreadful experiences.

"Bring him in here, Arden," X'andria said excitedly, when the story was over, "I may have found something." She stepped carefully back into the room where Ohlen held silent vigil over the lifeless man. With the others following close behind, she lay down on her back directly beneath the Elfish section of the ceiling.

"Put him right here, Arden." She patted the stone next to her left hand. "I don't know what this will do, but I'm pretty sure it will be good," and then she added quizzically, "and I'm nearly positive it won't be bad."

"What are you doing to me, X'an?" asked Gnome in a slightly worried tone.

"I'm so glad you asked!" X'andria brightened. "My theory is that the runes above us are in eight different languages. But I think they all probably relate to the same power, which is the power of life. The stuff growing in here was steeped in it because of these symbols. I didn't realize it right away, but," pointing now directly above her, "I can actually *read those*."

And with that, X'andria grabbed Gnome's wounded leg with a surprisingly tight grip, and a combination of otherworldly hisses, tones, and inhuman guttural noises began issuing forth from her mouth. Boudreaux and Arden looked on in awe from the doorway, and Gnome closed his eyes tightly in trepidation.

Bright, electric blue. With each word, the runes glowed

brightly, lifted from the stone, and floated toward her in space leaving the ceiling blank behind them. This was power. In any normal circumstance to utter just one of these words would have felt like ripping out a part of her body and mind. But she was not tearing this power out from within herself, she was merely activating it from where it was sealed above her. The air became thick with intention. This was a complex recipe of universal ingredients, each new word swirling more energy into a spinning vortex above her. *Two more words. One more word.*

And that was it. She had said them all. The last of the Elfish runes glowed and lifted from the arched ceiling. The vortex spun faster. And for one more moment, X'andria had the impression that this whole business of reading magic runes was easier than pulling on the power stored within herself. But then it happened. The mass of spiraling energy dove out of the ether and plowed directly down into her little body, which arched dramatically, glowed brightly, and lifted several feet off the ground. In recalling this moment, the best she could say was that it was simply ten times more indescribably intense than any other word she had used before, magnified once for each of the ten runes she had released.

Power coursed through X'andria's arm and into Gnome's prone body. He shot straight into the air with a jolt like he had been hit by lightning. Arden's cloak fell away, and Gnome landed on his feet, totally exposed.

The leg was fine. Never better. In fact, Gnome felt absolutely fantastic in every way. If Boudreaux and Arden had blinked they would have missed the slashes and gouges knitting themselves closed and the pigment of Gnome's skin swimming from blotchy bruises and scrapes back to his healthy, smooth monochrome.

X'andria lay gasping for breath and clutching her stomach. Her torch rolled on the stone floor beside her. On the other side of the pool, Ohlen's eyes clicked suddenly open, and so did those of the mysterious man lying beneath him. Boudreaux and Arden stared open-mouthed at the inexplicably restored Gnome, and Gnome looked straight past them, at the far wall of the adjacent room, and said matter-of-factly, "Hey everybody, what's that?"

The narrow streams plunged down noiselessly into two huge basins made of gold-veined rough stone atop the dais.

Chapter Twenty-Eight
DWARVES

"I was gonna ask *you* that," Boudreaux fired back, his eyes fixed suggestively on Gnome's naked midsection. Then, in a wholly different tone, he added, "X'andria, that was...unbelievable. Are you alright?"

"Very funny, *Bardo*," seethed Gnome, scrambling to cover himself with Arden's cloak. "But I was talking about the little seam on the wall right behind your big stupid head. I think we may have ourselves another door."

"I'm alright," X'andria panted, wincing and squeezing her eyes tightly closed. "That was totally amazing." And then, "What door, Gnome?"

"Yeah, I don't see anything," called Arden from the other room, having followed Gnome's gaze and gone to investigate.

Chapter Twenty-Eight

Ohlen broke in, "Friends, we have a new visitor." His voice was somehow even deeper and richer than usual. He had been so silent for so long, that his words instantly commanded everyone's attention.

"Friend or foe?" queried Boudreaux, his tone dangerous. Gnome's huge eyes narrowed suspiciously.

"Friend, I think; but why don't we ask him?" With visible effort, Ohlen removed his hand from the man's forehead and said softly, "Welcome back."

X'andria sat up and lifted her torch. Arden returned. Gnome and Boudreaux crowded in close, and Ohlen continued, "If you can manage it, we would like to know a little bit about who you are and how you came to be here."

"Who I am?" the man repeated slowly in a small and feeble voice. "It's so strange," he paused, "but I don't even think I know."

There was a long silence.

"Would it help you remember," Boudreaux used his most honey-sweet dulcet tone, "if I held your face underwater for a minute or two?"

X'andria swatted Boudreaux's arm, Gnome gave him a withering "Die now" expression, and even Ohlen managed a look of alarmed disapproval.

"Geoffrey," the man managed. "My name is Geoffrey. Of that I am certain. I had a life, but it was long ago, and at this moment I cannot see where I went or who I was."

They introduced themselves. Gnome wrung out his clothes, dressed, and offered Arden's cloak to Geoffrey. Geoffrey remained largely silent and despondent while they discussed a great many things, ate what little victuals that remained, and drank surprisingly fresh-tasting water from the pool.

Ohlen described his journey within Geoffrey's psyche, and X'andria filled them in on her interpretation of the magic power stored in the room's eight-paneled dome. Gnome and Boudreaux shared their experiences with what seemed to be another, higher portion of the same dwarf-made edifice, and they struggled for words to describe the statue's eyes.

Arden and Boudreaux asked Gnome again and again about the Westoveran prisoners, and seemed anxious to be reassured they had made it to safety. That brought them all to the inevitable discussion of what to do next.

"The issue is Ruprecht," said Ohlen heavily. "If he had not been taken, I would probably recommend we abandon this dark place, or return another time with an army behind us."

"Oh we *have* to rescue Ruprecht!" entreated X'andria. "We can't possibly leave him in this dreadful place."

"I'm just saying that the thing up there with the eyes is a whole new level of bad," Boudreaux persisted. "Gnome saw it too, and Ohlen, I'm sure that's behind whatever you've just been through inside Geoffrey's head here." Gesturing now at their newest member, "And who's to say, even if we do get Ruprecht back, that he won't come out a vegetable like this guy did?"

This earned Boudreaux another swat from X'andria and a fresh round of admonishments from the others.

"We're going in," said Arden firmly. "We don't leave our friends behind and that's it. I don't think this is a discussion about *if*, so much as it's a discussion of *how*."

"You have no obligation to assist us, Boudreaux," Ohlen's rich voice resonated in the stone chamber. The words hung heavily in the air.

"Yeah," added Gnome acidly, "it's not like you *owe* us anything."

185

After an awkward silence, Boudreaux began, "I don't think..."

X'andria, who had been staring at the ground—her thick red hair spilling forward to completely obscure her face—looked up at Boudreaux and studied his eyes, the faintest frown pulling at the corners of her mouth.

"I don't think I could live with myself," Boudreaux concluded emphatically, "if I don't help you recover your friend." He grinned toothily at each of them in turn.

"Here's what **I** think," said Gnome, shaking his head. "The action is clearly here in the dwarf palace. This is where the evil statue is, and this is where we're sure to find Ruprecht. The only other way in that we know of is through that tunnel Boudreaux and I went down. But I think that's a pretty exposed approach—putting the goblin lair behind us, and who-knows-what in front of us. I would bet that the second secret door right over there," pointing into the other room, "will take us into a lower wing of the dwarf palace and that, from there, we'll be able to assess the situation, and possibly approach from a better vantage point."

Ohlen explained to Geoffrey that he had three choices. He could stay with them and walk into certain danger, stay here indefinitely, or risk his luck on his own trying to escape through the goblin tunnels. In a surprisingly quick and firm decision, Geoffrey said he would like to come with them, and mumbled something about repaying their kindness.

Gnome's secret door was of precisely the same size and workmanship as the door X'andria had spotted from the tunnel. It was located on the opposite wall, and was totally undetectable to everyone else in the party except X'andria, even after Gnome showed them where it was.

They packed their few remaining belongings, drew what weapons they had, and pushed into the unknown through the dwarf-sized, perfectly weighted, sliding stone portal.

Arden was first. Carrying X'andria's torch, he ducked through the low opening. The space they entered was so narrow that he nearly collided with a sheer stone structure just a few feet from the aperture. Proceeding left, the only way possible, he came to the edge of the narrow passage and saw that the wall they had encountered was formed by the back of a grand marble dais at the end of an enormous room. The concealed door they had emerged from, therefore, was not only set invisibly into the wall, but was located in a tiny darkened passageway that would itself be easy to miss. Whoever built this place had not wanted the magical secret rooms to be found.

The large, still room had unlit torches in brackets spaced evenly throughout. Arden set about lighting them one by one. As light filled the hall, so too did his wonder at the spectacular beauty of the place. Deep veins of red, green and black swirled in the marble floors. Two huge polished columns stood astride short but wide double doors made of ornately carved hardwood with massive iron fixtures. Even the hardware surrounding the torches showed intricate craftsmanship with fine metallic filigree.

The flowing water fascinated X'andria. Her sharp ears heard the gently rushing sound as soon as they pushed into the dark space. Emerging into the open room, with Arden's illumination, her attention was drawn to two perfect needles of water streaming out of ornate mouths high up in the ceiling. The narrow streams plunged down noiselessly into two huge basins made of gold-veined rough stone atop the dais. The water spilled over the edges of the basins and fell into linear grooves cut into the wide steps. At the base of the structure, the grooves continued out into the floor, and converged in a small gold-rimmed pool located in the very center of the room. Transfixed, X'andria knelt by the nearest groove, placed a finger in the icy water, and smiled to herself as she watched the rapidly flowing liquid pool and run slightly over the perfect edges before removing her finger and letting it on its way.

Desolation. This place has known disaster, invasion, and neglect, thought Ohlen, as soon as the stale air filled his lungs and fine dust plumed beneath his feet. Ohlen quieted his eyes and ears, reaching out instead with his heart and mind. There was great unrest here. Many souls seemed locked in the cold stone, unwilling to depart, bitter and angry at the savage intrusion, outraged at the befouling of their sacred space.

Geoffrey trudged silently along, unseeing. His brain whirred to make sense of his life. There were memories but they swam together in misalignment. His life was a puzzle with no pieces that fit together. But he kept trying. *I am a good person*, he repeated to himself. While the particulars eluded him, he felt he had lived a principled existence. One thing he knew for certain, however, was that his former life had been torn apart.

Gnome fixed on the bodies. Dwarves. There must have been dozens of them. Mostly skeletons now, some with dry parchment-like skin stretched taut across their bones. Spears and arrows protruded at odd angles from some of them, while others had limbs severed, or nearly so, their arms, legs, and necks at impossible angles. Gnome did not generally like dwarves, but the slaughter here was brutal and tragic, and the injustice of it made him furious to his core.

The dwarves had defended their sacred home to the last breath, and their broken bodies littered on the floor, on the steps of the dais, on the great wooden table, and near the enormous doors, were a testament to their dedication and sacrifice.

Whoa, thought Boudreaux, *what's this? There is definitely a bunch of stuff I can use in here!* Everyone knew that dwarf-made weapons and armor were the best money could buy. *Looks like it's time to go foraging*, Boudreaux thought grimly. He quickly scanned the many fallen bodies, almost all of which still wore armor and clutched weapons of various kinds. *The only problem with dwarf stuff is that it's all so damn small!*

Boudreaux bounded up the steps of the dais to the largest of the dead dwarves. There he found a great silver helm with ornate script encircling its brim, and a small red ruby inset at the very top. *Good thing dwarves have big heads*, he thought, as he tried it on. But what had really attracted him was a full-sized broadsword. *Good thing dwarves are so strong*, he smiled to himself. *This fellow must have needed two hands to wield this monster.* Then he added sincerely, *Thank you, my friend. With this, you shall be avenged.*

"These would be perfect for *you*, X'andria," Arden called from the far side of the long wooden table. As she bounced over to him, he unbuckled and pried thick leather pads from the legs and torso of one of the desiccated dwarf bodies.

Gnome stooped over a small shrunken form, attracted by silver shining tubular guards on its forearms. *I am so sick of my arms getting sliced and stuck*, he thought. He grasped one of the bracers and tried to pull it free. Free it came, but the arm detached, emitting a dry audible crunch. Shaking the debris free, Gnome was delighted to find that the bracers fit him perfectly.

Under normal circumstances, Ohlen would not have approved

of pillaging the dead. His personal code of ethics led him to give away most of what he earned in life and strictly forbade him from stealing from another, dead or alive. While he recognized that some in his party did not live life by his moral standards, he often still allowed himself vocal disapproval of what he considered to be violations of decency.

But this was different. He could not be sure, but his firm belief was that the departed dwarves actually *wanted* them to take these belongings. He could feel their presence in the room. He knew their tragedy and empathized with their sadness. As his party peeled clothing from the dead, looked through bags and robes for precious items, tried out various weapons, and flipped over dry bones of the fallen as though looking through rugs at a bazaar, Ohlen got the distinct feeling that the departed souls cheered them on.

Ohlen's feelings were not often wrong. He strode over to the pool in the center of the room, kicked off his boots, placed his feet in the cool water, sat on the golden rim, closed his eyes, and meditated.

His eyes grew wide and his mouth snapped shut in terror
as a huge mucous-covered tentacle slithered up from below.

Chapter Twenty-Nine
BLAME

Imbeciles! How could you let them get away? They were mine. **Mine!** *And now you've lost them.*

Goblins crowded together in the cavernous room, shifting nervously, heads bowed. The eyes had summoned them, and now the voice berated them at their defeat.

Thag! Come forth. Explain yourself.

Bustling forward, a fat, squat goblin cowered before the tall, hooded figure: the source of the voice. The figure's right hand extended, and Thag was crushed forcibly to his knees with his metal hardware clanging on the stone and his bones issuing an audible crunch.

Thag licked snot from his nose and lips and stared fixedly at the ground.

Chapter Twenty-Nine

The eyes bore into his memory. *Thag was running from fiery serpents. He escaped! He saw the fleeing prisoners. He ran after them. He called to his cohorts. They fell in behind him. A small dark creature exploded out of the shadows into his feet and he fell. The others fell. They squirmed. Borog screamed. The creature lived and it was piercing them! They hurt it. Clawed it. Made it bleed. But it was so small and so fast. It shot away and disappeared again in shadow. He ran, but could not find it.*

All these memories bled painfully and unwillingly from his mind. His shame mounted as the eyes looked cruelly on at the evidence of his failure, at his defeat at the hands of a creature half his size.

You disappoint me, Thag! Who should pay for this, Thag? Someone must pay.

Thag turned wildly around and pointed at his nearest compatriot. An old bearded goblin who looked fearfully down at his navel like the rest of the clan.

Grot should pay! The voice jeered triumphantly. *Oh I agree, Thag. Grot was not even there, but I think he most certainly should pay, and pay dearly.*

Hearing his name uttered in his own mind caused Grot to try and run away. But he did not get very far. Thin black ropes issued like whips from the hooded figure's fingers and wrapped swiftly around the old goblin's ankles, causing him to fall roughly onto his face.

A ravenous roar emanated from beneath them. The earth shuddered. Grot was pulled by unseen hands backward across the floor, squealing and wetting himself, leaving a shiny trail smeared behind him.

She's hungry, Thag. Very hungry, and Grot is just the juicy morsel she needs. Look everyone, the show is about to begin.

The heads of the sorry gaggle of goblins snapped jerkily upward and their eyes were pinned on the helpless Grot as he was dragged screaming and clawing to the edge of a large hole broken into the stone floor in the middle of the room.

Boom. Boom. Boom. The floor shook beneath them.

Grot was balanced precariously on the edge of the pit. His eyes grew wide and his mouth snapped shut in terror as a huge mucous-covered tentacle slithered up from below. When it touched him his skin hissed and steamed, and his renewed wailing reached a fever pitch before he disappeared out of view with a snap.

Silence. Despair. Shame. Fear. They dared not move.

She's still hungry, Thag. The voice needled on cruelly.

*But perhaps I'll let **them** decide who's next.*

And with that, the hooded figure turned and glided swiftly away, releasing the goblins from their stasis. Thag, his broken knees unresponsive to his impulses to flee, had no chance. Whether retribution for the false and unfair blame he placed on Grot, or, more likely, out of fear for their own hides, the goblins rushed to him, still prostrate on the floor, and flung him bodily into the pit to join poor Grot and whatever hideous monstrosity lurked in the deep.

The dim light revealed more of the terrible story to their straining eyes.

Chapter Thirty
FORWARD

The party did not smell good. They smelled musty and sour as decayed death. But at least they were clothed, protected, and armed. Boudreaux, heedless of Ohlen's disapproval, packed a bag he found with precious metal objects and gems he'd pried from their fittings, and Gnome and X'andria surreptitiously snuck valuables into their own bags and pockets anytime they thought they were not being watched. Even Geoffrey allowed himself to be clad in thick leathers and a pair of boots that were over-large but would offer effective protection.

They crept silently from the great hall, cracking the huge doors slightly ajar, listening intently, and filing slowly out into the darkness.

Ohlen left the dwarf hall heavier than when he entered. He was filled with a new resolve. The spirits of the dwarves were traveling with him now, they moved in the walls that they and their ancestors had carved, and they moved within Ohlen himself. He was heavy not with burden and fatigue, but rather power-laden like a warship.

I was a protector, realized Geoffrey, suddenly. Walking into what was surely a dangerous situation brought out in him a strong desire to protect his new friends. This feeling was a familiar one to him, and with it came comfort and purpose.

Crunch!

Arden, in front and nearly blind in the dark, stepped on something that exploded noisily into pieces beneath his heavy boots.

Everyone stopped. They listened. They heard nothing.

Until the squealing.

High-pitched wailing echoed through the stone tunnels from afar. It carried on for about a minute before stopping as abruptly as it had begun.

"Light?" X'andria breathed.

"Yes," someone replied.

She had snuffed out and pulled an extra torch from the great hall to bring alongside her remaining travel torch. She quickly relit the dwarf torch, and the dim light revealed more of the terrible story to their straining eyes.

Arden's boot had obliterated the skull of one of dozens more murdered dwarves strewn throughout the long corridor. It was clear now that their home had been invaded, that they had retreated under attack, and had fought and lost their remaining lives in the great hall. Behind him, Ohlen now saw that the exterior of the beautiful wide wooden doors had been gouged and splintered by many violent attacks before being forced open by the enemy.

"I'll lead," said Gnome resolutely. "It's time to end this."

With X'andria's light defying the deep pressing darkness,

Gnome chose careful steps forward through the tangle of disintegrating remains.

They passed darkened rooms and passageways, but the squeals had come from further away and Gnome chose not to stop and investigate. Several minutes later, they found themselves in a grand hall with a wide staircase, and they saw that theirs was not the only source of light. Three large arches lined the landing atop the steps, and light poured forth from the one in the center. X'andria quickly extinguished the torch she was holding.

"Wait here," whispered Gnome, and he disappeared into the gloom.

They heard no sound. No noise came from above, none from behind, and none from Gnome.

As they stood huddled in silence, looking expectantly at the glowing archway above, facts began to click together in Geoffrey's muddled mind. *I lived in many homes*, he realized, *That is the reason for all the fragments and visions. I lived for many years, and knew countless souls. I know I am a protector and I know I am a healer and...* Geoffrey's mind again swam deliriously...*and I know you, oh great one.*

"That's the room, alright." They heard Gnome before they saw him materialize in front of them. "There's a big hole in the floor I hadn't seen before, and one of those hooded creeps is in there. I bet he'll know where Ruprecht is, but it might take some special convincing to get it out of him. Whatever you do, though, don't look at the statue."

"Did you see into hell?" Boudreaux asked ominously.

"What are you talking about?" Gnome replied.

"Hell," Boudreaux repeated. "When I looked in there, right in front of the statue, there was a big doorway into hell."

Chapter Thirty

Gnome considered this a moment. The group waited tensely for his answer.

"I wonder if *that's* what it is?" Gnome finally returned. "There was something that looked a little strange. Kind of wavy or blurry? I was trying not to look at the statue, though, so I didn't study it too closely. Is that what you're talking about?"

"You two are describing a portal to another world," X'andria burst in with barely contained enthusiasm. "If that's what it is, that's totally crazy!" Then, realizing no one around shared her excitement, she continued in a more measured and studied tone, "I can imagine how on one side you'd be able to see into it, but on the other it might just look like a ripple in space. They're incredibly rare! I wouldn't touch it, though: my understanding is they generally only go one way."

"What do we do, Gnome?" asked Arden.

"We go up there, avoid the pit, the statue, and X'andria's crazy space door, and make that guy tell us where Ruprecht is."

"But how do we handle him? I don't want to get hit with those damn black oily things again. I promised myself," Arden whined.

"I've got something that should stop him for at least a little while. You'll just have to buy me about ten seconds once we get in there," X'andria said coolly. "Let's do this."

Gnome glimpsed the monstrosity first.

Chapter Thirty-One
THE BATTLE BEGINS

The party moved stealthily across the open space and mounted the stairs, careful not to make a sound. Boudreaux and Arden were in front, shielding X'andria behind them. Gnome planned to skirt the perimeter of the room and do his best to be unseen once attention was drawn to the others. Geoffrey and Ohlen crept side by side at the rear of the party.

Arriving at the landing, they lingered momentarily in the shadow just beyond the light emanating from the room. The hole in the floor looked as though it had erupted from beneath. It was definitely not a feature placed there by the expert miners and masons of the dwarves. The dark hooded figure floated motionless just beyond the pit, in a state of suspended animation. Upon seeing him, Ohlen's breath grew short, and his skin crawled with icy spiders. The atmosphere of evil consumed his senses.

They all assiduously avoided looking at the statue and the wavy space toward the center of the great room, and for that reason, they also did not look closely at the hole in the far wall where they knew the goblin tunnels intersected with the majestic underground palace.

Ten seconds is all she needs thought Boudreaux, heart racing, as he and Arden rushed into the space and did their best to form a wall between X'andria and the hooded figure across the gaping hole. Gnome was away to the edge of the room like a flash.

The black hood raised slightly. X'andria's incantation began, and Arden and Boudreaux braced to be hit by more of the black snaky bonds. They did not expect, however, the volley of arrows that showered down upon them from their left, from near the goblin tunnel.

Arrows clattered to the hard floor around them. One lodged in the armor of Arden's left arm and another glanced off Boudreaux's new helmet. Another caught X'andria's left leg. It pierced clear through her thigh and her pinned robes quickly became wet with blood.

Her incantation ceased with a whimper, as her wounded leg buckled.

Fire again, they heard. But it was not their ears that heard it. The hateful voice, which scraped and hissed more than it spoke, seemed to erupt directly inside their minds.

Geoffrey was hit in the second volley. He grunted involuntarily as the point fractured the bone in his upper arm. Arden was also hit again. This time the arrow snuck through the chain mail covering his left leg and just pierced the skin beneath.

"Stay with her," Boudreaux ground out, and he raced toward the goblin archers.

Boom. Boom. Boom.

The floor began to shake, and a terrifying low roar, the sound of something huge, emanated from within the jagged hole.

Ohlen's brain screamed. His mind played tug-of-war with his

consciousness, the spirits of his compatriots, and their enemies. Still a bigger evil pulled on him, dared him to engage. And it laughed at him.

Gnome glimpsed the monstrosity first. He was creeping around the edge of the room toward the dark-robed man when the first of the grayish-white mucilaginous tentacles flailed above the broken edge of the pit. Frozen in horror, he witnessed what must have been a dozen slithering appendages flop onto the floor and strain high into the air as though looking for something, anything to ensnare and probe. Mucous flipped in huge drops all over the floor, and hissed in steamy clouds on contact with the stone. The tentacles were but a preview to the horror itself.

It must have been twenty feet long or more—Gnome couldn't see it all. The thing was an enormous, many-legged, segmented worm. Its huge sightless head had a fanged mouth rimmed with the wildly wriggling, slimy tentacles. At first, Gnome thought it was heading straight for him. He got the distinct sense that the tentacles themselves could smell, and that they had caught the sweet scent of gnomish flesh. But just then it maneuvered around, lumbering and quivering, to face Arden and the rest.

Get yourself together, dammit! X'andria's hands were covered in blood. More arrows had clattered around her. Boudreaux was gone. Someone else was hit behind her. From the floor, she could no longer see her primary target because the world's largest disgusting drippy worm had emerged from the giant hole and seemed very hungry. *Of course it did.*

Stealing a glance after Boudreaux, she saw he cut one goblin in half at the midsection with his enormous new sword, and was engaging two more. But three archers behind him were notching more arrows.

Chapter Thirty-One

Eyes, my pretties. She focused. Her slick fingers pulled three of her prized darts from within her robes and she lay them side by side on her outstretched palm. She saw the archers clearly, saw them clutching their faces, saw the blood spraying between their stubby fingers, and she said the word. *Tir'yavlie.* Fly.

Whoosh. The darts flew swiftly from her hand, propelled by some unseen force, and sank deeply into her chosen targets. The act left X'andria gasping and staring up once more at the horror towering above her.

Boudreaux had been expecting to take at least one arrow. They weren't great shots, but the three lined up to fire at him were so close, even they could not possibly all miss him. *I hate arrows—cowards' weapons*, he thought bitterly as he grit his teeth and pushed another unfortunate goblin off the hilt of his sword.

But it would not be a goblin arrow that hit him. At that moment, X'andria's magically propelled darts embedded themselves in all three archers, causing them to double over and drop their weapons in unison. What did hit him, however, was a weaponless goblin combatant who rushed forward from his right and leapt, claws-first, at Boudreaux's face.

Its attack was unexpected, and distracted slightly by the archers, Boudreaux did not have time to properly react. Before he knew it, he had been knocked over, and found himself fighting to keep his eyes from being gouged out and his nose from being bitten off by the slobbering assailant.

Arden had never imagined Mother Nature could create a beast so foul as the monstrous tentacular worm that now menaced them. Some part of it had emerged from the hole in the floor and rested on caterpillar-like legs; the rest was still below. While Arden didn't know anything about this creature, he most certainly understood the role of legs for all beings that had them.

His plan was simple. *Cut off the legs.* Maybe its own weight will drag it back into whatever foul abyss it came from. Arden rushed forward.

Meanwhile, Ohlen's mind raced. Their plan had been for X'andria to immobilize the evil man. They had not accounted for goblins and a giant hellish beast of the deep. Of the two things, the beast of the deep was the greater imminent threat to X'andria, and so Ohlen drew his sword and raced to assist Arden.

In a corner, Geoffrey had gone catatonic. Chaos reigned around him. They were all going to die. Seeing the black-robed figure, hearing that horrible voice—*that voice!*—it sent him into a deep dark spiral that even the arrow cutting through his left arm could not interrupt. The pain his body felt was nothing at all compared to what he had been through, to what lay in store for all of them. Beneath the fear, however, perhaps because of it—something ancient and comforting began to stir within him.

Alright, you little creep. Boudreaux finally had things under control. He grabbed and broke a goblin wrist, he punched hard and deep into stomach and ribs. Bile and snotty slobber ejected onto his face from the creature atop him before he rolled it off onto the floor. *Disgusting!* Boudreaux regained his feet, and launched the cringing goblin off to his right without thinking. It sailed through the air. It sailed, in fact, through the ripple in space. For all Boudreaux knew, it sailed straight into hell.

Without realizing it, Boudreaux had backed up almost all the way to the strangely-shaped portal. And he couldn't help himself. As the goblin faded from view, Boudreaux looked away from the mouth of hell, and found himself staring instead directly into the glowing eyes of the demon statue.

Boudreaux instead stood facing himself.
A double fully-armed and ready to attack.

Chapter Thirty-Two
THE OTHER BOUDREAUX

Burning eyes. The statue was frightful to be sure. Massive clawed hands protruded from beneath huge, folded bat-like wings. A powerfully muscular torso and neck supported a cruel head with saber-like teeth extending out from both upper and lower jaws like razor-sharp tusks. But all that faded quickly away as Boudreaux was gripped wholly by the hungrily probing eyes.

Boudreaux quickly lost awareness of the world around him. He did not notice the remaining goblin assailant warily approach him. Did not feel when it inserted a dagger unchallenged into his midsection. Did not flinch as the blood began to flow out of him and onto his legs and the white stone floor below.

Boudreaux was in another place now. What was this place? It was familiar. It smelled musty. There was the sweetness of oats, and the sour of manure. Both soiled his rough, dry hands. He was so small. Boudreaux was back home. Young and not yet muscular. Weak.

Large spiders wove webs here near the animals. He hated those spiders and he was terrified of them. In the morning, he'd open the door to the stables and use the handle of his shovel to sweep away the webs as far as he could reach without sticking any part of him into the dark. There were always new webs. Sometimes the heavy, furry dark bodies would plop out of the air when he did this, and scuttle away quickly into the shadows.

Boudreaux hated going in there, but his master made him fill the grain barrel whenever it was empty. Nerves tingling, blood like ice, he would run, not walk, to the dark grain pile and fill his shovel, before racing back to the safety of the light to deposit the meager offering into the huge barrel. It took many terrifying trips to fill the barrel.

Only once had a spider landed on his back when he was deeper in the darkness of the grain room. He was ten or so trips into refilling the barrel when he felt the impact of the deadly urchin on his back. It moved instantly, rapid little pricks on his soft skin rushing up toward the back of his neck. His already-charged nerves screamed. He jumped and thrashed; he yelled; he dropped his shovel, spraying grain everywhere, and bolted for the waning daylight.

His master was with the horses. He had been carousing with his friends. When they saw Boudreaux rush from the barn screaming, Boudreaux's master went to investigate. Upon finding the spilled grain, he grew irate and tied Boudreaux to a tree. The men took turns lashing him with the long whip normally reserved for taming the wildest of the horses. The small boy cried and bled silently as they laughed and had another round.

But that was not the worst of it. The worst of it was being locked for the night in the grain room with the spiders, his shivering little body slick and sticky with blood. That was the night he decided to run away. He vowed to someday be so powerful that nothing like this could ever happen to him again.

So why was he back here now? Why was he so small? Why was his master calling him from outside? Had the whole thing been a dream? Had he never left?

His master was coming. The keys were jingling at the door. His master called to him. Boudreaux uncoiled his nearly naked body in the terrifying darkness and risked a few steps toward the door, expecting at any moment for his face to encounter a taut web and a mess of wriggling legs and pincers.

Light! The door was open. He ran for it.

Boudreaux emerged, fully-grown now, into a dim, grey, foggy clearing. The barn and the animals were gone. But his master still called to him, still mocked him, still challenged him. Turning to face the voice, however, Boudreaux was stunned to find it was not his master at all.

Boudreaux instead stood facing himself. A double fully-armed and ready to attack.

Weaponless, Boudreaux dodged the assault, rolling swiftly away.

"I don't want to fight," he said. "Who are you?"

Flashing steel was the only answer he received. He narrowly avoided being badly wounded, and escaped with a small nick, which turned into a thin red line of blood.

This is a dream! Boudreaux realized. *I'm in some terrible dream.*

Chapter Thirty-Two

But it appears to be a dream in which I can bleed. And if I can bleed, then he can bleed. Which is, I suppose, really me bleeding, but I'd rather it was him than me.

The doppelganger did not have Boudreaux's moves, thankfully. It had been created in his mold and, no doubt, possessed his speed and power, but whoever or whatever was piloting it, did not seem to understand how to use his attributes to best advantage.

They danced for some time. Boudreaux watched and learned, rolled and ducked. He took two direct and painful hits, one to his arm, the other to his chest.

Eventually he saw an opening. The other Boudreaux committed over-much. His lunges took him ever so slightly off balance. Boudreaux slowed to bait his opponent, and at the last instant rolled left just as the lunge came at him. He sprang and grappled from behind. *God, I'm strong*, he thought, as he strained against powerful and violent countermeasures.

Just when he thought he might lose his hold, he caught the assailant's right foot with his own, tripped him, and they tumbled heavily to the misty ground. It was the moment he'd been waiting for. He took a chance and put all his effort into wrenching the sword from his own powerful grasp. A few punched and kicked and bitten seconds later, he managed to come away with the steel prize.

Turning immediately, he plunged the long sword deep into the other's heart. He saw outrage and disbelief in his own eyes. But they were not his eyes after all. These eyes glowed red. The eyes of the demon.

And with that, Boudreaux snapped out of it. He found himself face-to-face with the very same eyes, but now they were not nearly so scary, set as they were in an inanimate statue.

He became aware that his left leg was wet from blood seeping out of his gut. The goblin before him was eyeing him curiously, crimson dripping from its dagger, poised to insert it once more into Boudreaux's frozen frame.

But the goblin would not get that chance. Boudreaux was frozen no more.

*He bucked violently against her will like a
wild bull ferrying an unwelcome rider.*

Chapter Thirty-Three
THE BATTLE CONTINUES

Cutting off the giant worm's legs turned out to be surprisingly easy. The huge body was quite soft actually, and with Arden's great power and focus, he lopped off two of the stubby legs in one stroke.

The huge beast spewed puss-colored goo from the openings and lurched sideways off-balance. But its enormous head also turned to the source of its pain and two slimy tentacles slathered across Arden's armor and up the side of his face.

Wild strangled screams issued unbidden from Arden, like he had just fallen into red hot burning embers. It felt like acid was melting his face. Somehow through the sheer pain, he also perceived the hiss emitting from his searing skin and the steam rising from his armor as the acid rapidly ate it away.

Ohlen took Arden's lead. Seeing the huge beast veer off-balance at the loss of its right forelegs, he lunged to make it a symmetrical pruning. Viciously slashing, he hacked off the other front leg, and then proceeded to the one behind it. With bloody mucous pouring freely from both sides of its smooth body, the roaring flailing nightmare slid unwillingly back down beneath the stone rim.

Chapter Thirty-Three

Arden frantically stripped off his steaming, melting armor. Boudreaux, bleeding but reanimated, flung a second and final goblin through the dimensional portal. Gnome crept closer behind the black-robed figure. Ohlen raced to X'andria's side. Geoffrey leveled a strangely cool stare across the freshly deserted pit, lips working silently.

And fire poured in ten massive jets from the fingertips of the black-hooded man, swirling into a huge inferno over his head.

Geoffrey ran. This was his time. A chance to repay.

In a suspended moment, all of them—except Arden, who was totally absorbed with stripping off steaming articles of clothing—watched dumbstruck as Geoffrey raced around the gaping hole to confront the man and his fireball.

With a deafening hiss, the fireball flew toward them. The massive sphere expanded as it sped across the room, hungrily devouring air as it advanced. Nothing would survive this hellish inferno.

But then the unimaginable happened. Geoffrey spread his hands wide and an invisible wall sprang from him, stretching floor to ceiling, and separating the band from fiery death. They would not have been able to see the magical barrier had the impact of the fireball against it not caused the fire to explode and flatten outward in all directions in search of a way to get through and devour its intended targets. It was a remarkable sight, really, to view demonic fire expanding as though looking at it from behind clear glass. But X'andria was the only one in the right frame of mind to truly appreciate the magic as it happened.

Shuddering under the pressure of the attack, Geoffrey stumbled backward. As his shield dissolved and the fire dissipated, he lost his footing at the jagged edge of the pit, disappearing into the hole.

Everyone heard the audible squelch, and the agonized howl that followed. Ohlen sensed the departure of Geoffrey's troubled spirit, like a flickering light suddenly vanished.

The worm was gone, the goblins were gone, the giant wall of fire was gone, Geoffrey was gone...the robed figure was not gone. The dark menace was absorbed ominously in a complex series of arm motions, evoking some other elemental horror, so X'andria began her incantation in earnest once more.

Gnome jumped. He hit the black-robed man hard, feet first, in the middle of his back. *That's gotta hurt*, Gnome thought, landing upright and feeling quite satisfied with himself. The impact blew the hood off the man's head and caused him to fall forward onto all fours.

Ruprecht? Ohlen realized with a shock. He began to run forward.

Ruprecht worked to steady himself, his shiny eyes black as night. *This puny body is so weak!* He thought. *But it will have to do.* Black oil emerged from his fingertips like claws.

X'andria, still on the ground, held herself upright with her left hand and extended her right to point directly at Ruprecht as she finished the last of her words. *You will not move so long as I hold you*, she thought. *Ly'alobaqa'.* Stay. He bucked violently against her will like a wild bull ferrying an unwelcome rider. *So much power*, she thought, but her hold remained, her focus remained, and she knew she would have to keep it that way as long as she could maintain consciousness.

Which turned out not to be very long, actually. She saw Ohlen dive headlong onto Ruprecht, she saw them lock together, then X'andria saw no more. Her right arm fell, her left arm buckled, and her head crashed hard onto the cold stone floor.

I will destroy you, little man. But not before I use your body to bring ruin and pain to everything you love.

Chapter Thirty-Four
THE EYES

———————

Ruprecht's body opened up as before and the black abyss lashed out at Ohlen like a huge elemental viper. But Ohlen was ready this time: he was not the same Ohlen any more.

Ungodly power tore into him. It was full assault—it tried to wrench him apart. It pulled not on arms and legs, but rather on belief and memory. His spirit was submerged in a fathomless vat of evil and hate that searched relentlessly for weakness.

What do you want? It asked him. It showed him past loves. It showed him trinkets he wanted as a boy. It showed him terrible power, opulent wealth beyond anything he could imagine. But these were easy challenges for Ohlen. Ohlen had long ago mastered worldly temptation.

Then came the eyes. Such intensity. They burned so close to his own he could feel them inside him. They wanted to be inside his own eyes—to be his own eyes. *You think you are a match for me, little man?* They taunted. *Your friend is like paper, you are dry leaves, I am steel and fire and the essence of might itself.*

Let's talk about pain.

And the torment began. Every sense was assaulted at once. He smelled roasting death, he heard screams louder than any ears could withstand, his nerves exploded with anguish as he was compressed by impossible weight that would destroy any body in the physical plane.

The eyes mocked him. Reveled in his pain.

*Let's talk about **his** pain.*

Now Ruprecht was before him. Ohlen relived the scene of the bodily invasion by the black marble. Saw in slow detail the brutal cutting, whirring, and swimming of the terrible orb.

And Ohlen saw his chance. He willed himself to the marble. He leapt to it in his mind, grasped it with his fingers. *Come into me, if you dare,* he screamed, *take **this** body, if you are so powerful.*

As the marble entered him, liquefying his flesh in a spray of blood and tissue, his eyes filled with fire and his ears filled with laughter.

I will destroy you, little man. But not before I use your body to bring ruin and pain to everything you love. This, little man, will be something your sad soul will regret for all eternity.

And there he was. Back in the deep prison of his youthful training. Evil all around him, pressing in upon him. But this evil was far greater than any he had known as a boy. This was crushing, overwhelming. This was exactly what he had prepared for.

He pushed back. He found light and he found good. He saw X'andria's joy at knowledge and Arden's love of creatures great and small. He saw Ruprecht's selfless piety and Gnome's courageous heart. He saw Boudreaux's kindness beneath his crusty exterior, and he saw Geoffrey's ultimate sacrifice. These powers he brought together within himself, and they fueled his fight.

But it was not enough.

The laughter was terrible. It was terrible because it knew. It knew it would win. It knew his power, his limitations, his resources, and it knew how to easily overwhelm all of them with an evil so vast and so old that nothing in Ohlen's arsenal stood a chance against it.

He curled up in a little ball in his cold, grimy cell. He clung to the bright but fading ball of good within him, to his smiling friends and his shining heroes, as the black pushed in all around him, and crushed to dust the walls of his memory.

And Ohlen began to feel hopelessness. And with hopelessness came that faraway flicker of desire.

It was in that state they found him. The dwarves. Hundreds of them. Their spirits poured out of the small square of stone floor remaining around him and they pushed back against the black. They rebuilt the stone cell of his memory as only dwarves can do. They hammered and throttled the black void with the reckless abandon available only to those with nothing left to lose. And in their midst, swimming in their gratitude, steeped in the injustice of their demise and the power of setting things aright, Ohlen felt himself return. He felt his warmth restore. He joined with the many souls of the fallen, he shined with the brightest light of courageous good, and he banished the blackness, the fire, the hate, the greed, and the hideous mocking laughter completely from his soul.

And at that moment, the small black marble dropped from between Ruprecht and Ohlen's locked bodies, bounced once on the stone floor, and rolled to rest in silent stillness nearby.

To know that we are not alone.

Chapter Thirty-Five
AFTERMATH

There are those moments when we want something so badly, it feels like a heavy lead ball has lodged in our chests. It feels like our hearts will be crushed unless we get what we want. It's hard even to think about anything else. The feeling extends upward and tingles on our lips. We can almost taste the flavor of our wishes, even as our stomachs below gnaw hungrily on themselves in impatient longing.

Other times we lose precious dreams or hopes or people. They fade from us forever and we are confronted with the inexorable truth that we, too, will someday fade away. So we grieve. We face ultimate powerlessness when some vibrant presence shines before us one moment, only to be snatched away the next, and realize there is nothing we can do to change it. So a once-colorful space in our souls becomes a void that fills with the thick gray of grief.

Chapter Thirty-Five

Fortunate are those moments when caring hands are willingly extended to us. Hands that grasp our own and comfort us, lead us forward, guide us to safety or knowledge or wisdom or even happiness. And in those touches, in those moments, we make connection. If we are enlightened enough, if we can be vulnerable, we are able to feel genuine gratitude. And bathed in that light, we are lifted briefly to grasp that paradoxical will-o-the-wisp we search for our entire lives.

To know that we are not alone.

From this confused matrix of emotions, Ruprecht, embraced in Ohlen's arms, came gasping into the world reborn. Waves of desire, grief, and gratitude churned within him so vehemently as to lock out any cogency that may have otherwise settled his newly unfettered mind.

Gnome stood and surveyed the scene before him. The tangle of limbs that was Ohlen and Ruprecht lay still now. The whole room was eerily tranquil. The mayhem had given way to utter silence punctuated once by the distinct click of the hellish marble landing on the hard floor, and echoing faintly in the vast stone room.

In that frozen moment, Gnome saw Arden, stripped naked to the waist, looking aghast across the open pit at Ohlen and Ruprecht as if expecting some new menace to rise between them. One side of his face was a raw slurry of whitish red where the worm's acid tentacles had melted his skin.

Oh god, please let her be alive, Gnome thought, looking now at X'andria, motionless on the floor behind Arden, the arrow still sprouting out of her left leg.

Boudreaux examined his mid-section. Gnome could see only the top of his head, covered by the great dwarven helm Boudreaux now wore. The huge fighter stood starkly against a field of fallen goblins. His hands were also covered in blood, as he tried with his fingers to slow the bleeding of the nasty gash beneath his navel.

Gnome strained to hear sounds beyond the room. He hoped desperately that the danger was truly gone. He heard nothing. He felt no distant impact of steps radiating through the earth. Perhaps they had purged the hellish nest, or perhaps the remaining goblin cretins had fled with the incapacitation of their commander.

Gnome's shoulders relaxed.

His gaze met Arden's from across the ruptured pit. One clear blue eye, the other swimming in red, looked back at him, and Arden's wreck of a face broke from its cast of worry into a boyish grin.

Gnome grinned back. He was not alone. And he was deeply, deeply grateful for it.

They emerged into the light of day.

EPILOGUE

Exhausted though he was, Ohlen willed himself to carefully collect the black marble, herding it alongside its twin into his small ivory case.

"Arden," called Boudreaux from beside the statue, "don't look at it, but come over here and help me put *this* thing in *there*," he indicated the open pit. With much grunting and gnashing of teeth, the two powerful men slid the massive stone statue to the edge of the pit, and toppled it headfirst into the darkness. A muffled roar from far below told them it had landed on the foul crawling worm monster, and at the precise moment of impact, the wavy portal to the hellish dimension blinked out of existence.

"Let's get out of here," suggested Gnome. "Arden, can you take X'andria? Boudreaux, can you help Ruprecht? I'll lead the way."

EPILOGUE

Ohlen followed the others as usual. He reflected solemnly on Geoffrey. He reflected on the dwarves. He thanked them for believing in him, for saving his life and his soul. He was pretty sure he even sensed them returning the gratitude.

X'andria awoke partway through the goblin tunnels. Her leg was throbbing, and she had a splitting headache. "What happened?" she stammered. "You were awesome," Arden replied, wincing through the pain of moving his still-searing face, "and now we're leaving." A few steps later he elaborated, "You helped us get Ruprecht back, but then we killed your space door, sorry about that."

When they emerged into the light of day, Ohlen drank in the sunshine and beauty of life around him, but with it came keen awareness of the insatiable hunger he had felt in the profound darkness just behind them.

They tightly bound X'andria's leg and, with a little help, she was able to limp unaided. As they ambled along, she remained lost in thought: the fireball, the portal, the crazy black oily bonds, Geoffrey's amazing invisible shield, the runes and the singing pool—she wanted to understand it all. Her bright eyes glinted hungrily.

After setting her down and dressing X'andria's wounded leg, Arden asked if they could walk to Bridgeton. "I want to see Rowena again, and make sure Helga and the others escaped safely," he explained in a mix of hope and concern.

There were a few shops in Bridgeton that Arden wanted to visit as well. Having stripped off most of his clothing after the tentacle business, he was looking forward to getting some functional and stylish new garments. A famous healer was also said to reside near Bridgeton, and he hoped she might be able to restore his melted face.

No longer carrying X'andria, Arden dug hopefully into his field satchel for his precious wooden pipe, but was disappointed to find it broken into several pieces. *One more thing to buy in Bridgeton*, he thought as he gazed forlornly at the broken stem.

Pockets bulging and the way clear before him, Gnome's quick little strides were buoyed with a strong sense of belonging. Since emerging into the land of the big people, it was not until this moment that he felt truly at home among them.

Boudreaux smiled too, in spite of himself. He had been a loner for a long time. But mostly that was because so many people had let him down. This bunch had not let him down at all. Far from it. "Ah, Bridgeton," he sighed brightly to no one in particular. "I haven't been there in a long time. The mead at the Dancing Deer Inn is one of the best I've ever had, and the wench who served it," Boudreaux paused to find the right words, "well, she's one of the best I've ever had, too."

And then there was Ruprecht. Ruprecht had no words. He had returned, but he was not sure from where, exactly. The others chattered brightly along, but his experience had not been theirs.

He had done and seen terrible, terrible things.

Ruprecht absently cradled his tormented left hand. On he trudged because that's where his friends were going, because he lacked the wherewithal to do anything else.

But it was undeniable. A part of him wanted to turn right around and go back.

And coming Winter 2016

TINDER & FLINT

ROCKMOOR

By
Matthew Hinsley

Art by
Billy Garretsen

A special preview...

The boy became acutely aware of the chilly wind off the sea, the noisy insistent lapping at the shore, the bobbing of the ships.

Chapter One
MORDIMER

Mordimer was sweating. His voice was raw from ceaseless pleading. He spent the sleepless night alternately clawing his way around the cold, dark room in search of a way out, and clutching his wife and two daughters close to him for warmth and comfort. Together their voices rose and fell through the night like a sad, poorly rehearsed chorus of feral cats.

No answers came.

The question they kept asking the merciless walls, and the deaf ears beyond, was why. *Why did you take us? What do you want with us? What are you going to do with us?*

Mordimer was positively terrified. He was terrified for them. He had brushes with death before, and while he was not hoping to come face to face again any time soon, the thought of his own end was far more welcome than the injury or demise of his precious family. *Let them go!* was a regular refrain shouted throughout the damp hellish night, often followed or preceded by, *I'll do anything you want!*

Chapter One

He was a big man. He was, perhaps, most at home in the woods hunting or walking in silence. As a boy he learned to recognize the sounds and tracks of animals. He loved to follow his father on his excursions into the forest.   When he was orphaned at thirteen, Mordimer's size and gentle demeanor attracted the attention of other boys, particularly those inclined to violence. It took only a few beatings before he learned to use his size and instincts to defend himself.

Soon after his parents' death, in desperation, he found his way to the docks of Rockmoor. The docks and shipyards were the heart of commerce for the small port city. On the afternoon of his very first day there, a jovial and corpulent captain noticed the urchin skulking near a pile of fishy traps and salt-dried nets.

"Oh ho! What have we here?" he boomed, flapping and rolling his way to stop directly over the cowering youth. "Is there something here you'd like, boy?" his eyes glinted with worldly experience and a tinge of humor, his flowing scarlet and black silk garments billowing in the ocean breezes. "Maybe something your dirty little fingers are hoping to grab when Jastro isn't looking?"   The big jovial eyes narrowed and swept the piled items on the dock in mock accusation.

Mordimer was speechless. He was frightened. He had not taken anything. If he was honest, though, he had to admit his biting hunger had prodded him to notice the valuable things on the docks that seemed easily portable.

"Come now boy," Jastro relaxed the ruse of indignation in his voice and countenance, and allowed the faintest hint of sincerity to creep into his tone, "what is it that brings you here all by yourself?"

Perhaps it was hunger, or perhaps desperation. But in that moment Mordimer found courage to answer the opulent stranger directly. This was a chance, and he had not had too many of those in his short troubled life.

"A job, sir," he managed.

"A job!" cried the captain to the audience of seagulls and waves. "The boy wants a job," Jastro continued, feigning contemplation, "and where might your parents be, boy?"

"Mum and dad are dead, sir," Mordimer replied meekly.

Jastro considered this for several long moments during which time the boy became acutely aware of the chilly wind off the sea, the noisy insistent lapping at the shore, the bobbing of the ships, of the rigid dry mask of his own face as he squinted up hopefully at the loud seaman, the sun shining brightly above.

"I'll tell you what, boy," he rummaged in his enormous black sequined vest, "you be here tomorrow morning at first light and we'll see if I can find something to keep you occupied." And with that he pushed two small copper coins into Mordimer's limp hands with his warm, pudgy fingers, and strode off into the city.

The next morning, Mordimer woke early beneath the slatted wood boards of the docks. He was nervous and had slept poorly, not wanting to miss his early appointment. One of the copper coins had bought him a cup of powerfully fragrant fish stew, the other coin had joined him for his fitful slumber, nestled tightly in the same hand he used as a pillow.

Jastro emerged at first light from a large vessel with several strapping and exotic-looking elaborately tattooed men. He whistled to Mordimer with a beckoning flick of his wrist, and Mordimer raced to meet him. There was work to do. It was hard, heavy, sweaty work moving crates, carpets, fabrics, casks and other cargo. But it was perfect. Almost instantly Mordimer fell into the rhythm of the simple physical labor beside the wordless sailors.

When the sun set, Mordimer was exhausted, smelly, incredibly hungry, and extremely happy. Jastro gave him four more of the copper pieces and invited him back the following morning to clear the hold of another trading vessel. That evening the boy spent two of the coins on a larger bowl of stew and a hunk of bread. And over night he slept soundly, holding fast to the three copper pieces he had now saved.

Through this first employment Mordimer found other jobs loading and unloading goods of all kinds at the docks. But anytime Jastro was at port, he would drop everything to work for his mysterious benefactor. After several months he saved enough copper to rent a tiny room at a nearby inn, where he ate, slept, and carefully saved his earnings. On slow days he would leave the city and hunt in the dense lush forests of his youth. He often returned with the carcass of a deer or boar that he would skin and carve and then trade for some of the myriad treasures that flowed through the docks each day.

He met his wife one early fall afternoon when the nights were just becoming colder. He had several extra pelts stored in his room, and he knew that, with the cold air blowing in, he would be able to trade them well.

She sat on a blanket with a basketful of oysters in front of a dingy boat that looked barely seaworthy. A loud drunkard, her father, swayed on board and heaped derision on his other children. She stared mournfully at the ground as Mordimer approached. Mordimer was very fond of oysters, and while the whole basket wasn't worth even one of the pelts he carried, he fancied trying one very much. He was just thinking about how many coins he was carrying when she turned her gaze upward and looked deeply into his face with her huge almond-shaped eyes.

And that was it.

Taking note of the potential customer, her father became silent. When his daughter did not speak up immediately about their wares, he blundered from the boat and apologized to the stranger for his idiot-daughter's manners. He asked if the stranger might like some of the freshest oysters in all of Rockmoor. His voice growing louder and more insistent, as if hoping some other stray passersby might hear as well, he bragged about the secret place they caught these oysters, a place only he knew.

And Mordimer and the girl ignored him, lost in each other's eyes.

Finally the wiry little man lumbered toward them, rage in his drunken stare. The girl tore her frightened eyes away and cowered slightly as though expecting to be struck. Mordimer stepped forward and spoke up, "forgive me my manners, sir. I do love oysters and I admire great beauty, and I've found both at once right here before me. I'm overcome."

Light dawned in the man's polluted mind, "she's not for sale you sick city bastard. But for copper I'll gladly deal ya some oysters to take back wherever you come from."

For the second time in his life, Mordimer realized he was being given a chance. Chances, he had come to believe, were to be seized when offered.

"I wish to marry your daughter, if she'll have me." Her bewildered look of fear and excitement at his brash statement was one Mordimer would never forget. "I'm carrying four furs, twenty-two coppers, and eight silvers," at the word 'silvers' the man's jaw went slack, "and if she'll walk with me tonight I'll leave them all with you as a token of my good faith."

And, indeed, they eventually left together that night, Mordimer and Zarina. Navigating through the drunken depths of her father's greed, pride and anger was not easy. But the thought of freedom made Zarina's features sparkle with a whole new radiance, and Mordimer, emboldened by her looks of desperate enthusiasm, was prepared to win her at any cost. Much flattery, one threat, two rough exchanges, four furs, twenty-two coppers, and eight silvers later, the two walked quickly and awkwardly together from the swaying dock without even knowing each others' names.

Sometimes Jastro transported people. Zarina's eyes narrowed the first time Mordimer described it to her. They had two small children now, a bigger room, and a growing secret stash of valuables from their years of hard work and modest living. Mordimer respected Jastro, he trusted him, and even though they rarely spoke, he believed Jastro to be an honorable man. The conditions of the passengers were not always clean and comfortable, and they often looked beleaguered from their journey. *Who ever said sea voyage was easy?* he reasoned with Zarina. In truth, Jastro's crew dealt primarily with the passengers, who were often hurried into waiting carriages that trundled off into the narrow alleys of The Grotto, Rockmoor's southern borough by the coast. Mordimer just busied himself with the heavy traded goods, and decided at some point to stop talking to Zarina about the live cargo altogether.

His fingertips were bleeding now. The incessant searching and scratching, the hammering of his powerful arms on the heavy door and solid walls was taking its toll. Zarina and the girls were reduced to soft whimpers and quiet sobs.

And then, suddenly, the door opened and light flooded in.

Mordimer rushed the intruder. He had played this out in his mind all night long. *When the universe gives you a chance, you have to take it.* Just beyond the threshold were two people. One of them he recognized. His eyes grew wide in disbelief as he barreled forward toward him.

Even if he had not stuttered his steps in his moment of realization, Mordimer would have had no chance. In mid-flight a flash burst from within the dark crimson robes of the second, smaller, man and Mordimer instantly lost control of his body. He sailed forward and out the door on momentum alone, and landed with a limp flop on the cold floor beyond. He heard the door slam behind him, but could not turn to look. He heard the impact of Zarina's body against it along with her anguished shrieks as rough hands grabbed him under his armpits and dragged him away.

Mordimer's lifeless body would not respond to his screaming nerves. He could see and hear. He could think. On they went, through a network of quiet stone passageways, and down countless short flights of stairs, his feet bumping noisily along down each step.

At last they stopped. This place was lit by many candles. There were books and parchments and countless jars. They stood him up in a tall box, and fastened him upright tightly with thick straps at his shoulders, waist and ankles. Before him on the floor was an ornate rug. He had seen these rugs come off the trading vessels from time to time, he himself may have unloaded this very piece.

A low commanding voice emanated from beneath the crimson hood, and the big man who had dragged him here, the man he knew, knelt on the floor and slid the ornate rug away. Mordimer pleaded for mercy with his eyes. But the man was careful to keep his gaze averted.

Revealed beneath the rug, embedded in the stone itself, was an image resembling a black bat with ruby red eyes. Cold fear rolled over Mordimer.

The robed man was talking. He was hissing and grunting constantly now. He approached Mordimer's restrained and comatose body and tore open his tunic to reveal his powerful naked chest beneath.

Muttering louder now, the man placed a cold hand on Mordimer's heaving stomach. Mordimer's eyes roamed over the room. He saw animal and human skulls. He saw beakers of what was most assuredly blood. He could not be certain, but it seemed the eyes in the floor were glowing now, were looking back at him.

And now the robed man produced a long black serpentine blade. *Oh god no!* Mordimer screamed in his mind. He willed his thoughts, those that he knew would be his last, to his girls, and to his sweet Zarina. *This is it*, he thought, *my last chance, and I had better take it.*

And with his mind nestled in that sweet reverie, Mordimer's eyes saw his life's blood drain quickly from him in thick sheets onto the floor. Impossibly, his eyes saw the onyx inlay hungrily drink up every last drop, the rubies now blindingly bright. Heavily drooping now, his eyes saw the man in the crimson robes step back to him over the clean dry floor. Finally his eyes closed and he saw no more.

Until several minutes later, when they fluttered open once again.

But they were white now, and without pupils. The blank eyes stared straight ahead unblinkingly.

An exclusive Q&A
with the minds behind the new fantasy adventure series

TINDER & FLINT

We here at T&F HQ feel very lucky indeed to collaborate with artist Billy Garretsen for the illustrations that grace the cover, pages, and *tinderandflintbooks.com* website. His work vividly evokes the characters, the adventures, the gushy goblin parts in ways we hadn't imagined... And he somehow pulled it off between his post as UX Design Lead at upcoming massively multi-player online game, Crowfall (*www.crowfall.com*), and as a partner in the vampire role-playing online community, Shadow's Kiss (*www.shadowskiss.com*)— amongst even more projects! He'll be the first to admit that he doesn't sleep much. He's also fond of saying, "If you want something done, ask a busy person."

1) First off, the cover design is awesome. How did you come up with the concept?

I'm glad you like it! When I read the initial draft of *Tinder & Flint*, it felt like the beginning of a grand adventure and it reminded me of some of my favorite movie posters like Indiana Jones and the Star Wars series. These, and many others, were painted by art legend Drew Struzan. While my style is very different from his, he has been a tremendous influence on my composition and characters. For *Tinder & Flint*, I wanted to stage a few vignettes amidst large character portraits in this cinema style to portray some of that fun adventure feel from my youth. I don't know if Boudreaux was meant to be the leading character—but he was certainly the one that stuck out in my mind so I painted him the largest. I think in subsequent books, new characters will take the leading spot. And how could I not throw the giant worm monster in there? It is a small part of the story, but again, one that stands out.

2) What drew you to *Tinder & Flint*?

I am a fan of new challenges. I have done almost every creative role in the video game space, from artist to designer and even composer. I was drawn to the opportunity to try a different storytelling medium, as well as the opportunity to create a new illustrative style for myself.

3) What was your favorite aspect of illustrating the book? What was the most difficult part of it?

My favorite aspect was developing the chapter etchings. Some chapters utilize very iconic or abstract images to sum them up while others are more literal snap shots of action within. It was a bit of a game reading a chapter and then figuring out how best to capture it in a single image. Since the art and the text flow together, I was able to enhance the narrative pacing and in certain spots deliberately misdirect the reader. The biggest challenge of this project was coming up with all of these illustrations without a lot of visual reference for this world and its characters. Each etching was actually kind of like creating concept art. The first time I drew some of the characters they looked quite different from what ended up in the book. Though, as each new piece of art was made the characters started getting more identifiable. I think next time around, it will be much easier.

4) How did you grow as an artist with this project?

I think there are two ways I have grown: One, I feel like after creating the front and back cover paintings my confidence in digital painting has grown. Historically I have only dabbled in Photoshop, favoring the clean vector aesthetic of Adobe Illustrator. So in one very straightforward sense, I grew new Photoshop painting skills. While I have much room to improve, I am no longer intimidated by the tools and can now utilize them any time I need a more handmade, painterly look. Two, I grew as a visual storyteller through the chapter etchings. With each etching, I had to create an image to enhance the narrative so every detail had to matter. I had to really think about every line. This is doubly true when I could only work in black and white. This meant only relying on shape, contrast and contours to compose these story beats. I learned how to better balance the details, guide the eye and leave some room for reader interpretation. The first few were a real struggle but after a handful, it was easy to get in a groove and by the end of the book, the etchings were coming out in half the time.

5) We've heard that you played drums in a metal band and like you mentioned, even composed music for video games. Did you have a song, rhythm, or soundtrack in your head (or playing) as you worked on the etchings? What were they?

I have an eclectic taste in music when I work and most times the criteria is simply that it needs to have a good beat. Some nights I would listen to game soundtracks and others more mainstream electronic stuff like Prodigy. As far as getting in the mood I did have Lord of the Rings and the Hobbit playing on a second monitor for many of the art sessions. Oddly, I don't listen to rock and metal all that much anymore even though I played that style for many years. I am regressing back to my '80s youth of drum machines and fat synths. I don't think there is a correlation between what I hear and what I draw, really. Just whatever sounds good and gets me focused.

6) If you were stuck on a deserted island, which two 80s cartoon characters would you like to hang out with?

Tough one! Just two? That's only half of the Ninja Turtles, what are you doing to me?! In that case, I would take Optimus Prime and Panthro from the Thundercats. I figure a giant transforming robot and a genius mechanic are a good combo to take on an adventure. I don't imagine having to rough it for very long before we put our heads together and come up with some fancy schmancy bro spa. Then we can all sit around the sauna and talk trash about Bumblebee.

Q & A

Speaking of busy people...

By day, Matthew Hinsley runs an arts non-profit organization, teaches Arts Administration at the University of Texas-Austin, and shares musical discovery through his private classical guitar studio. By night, he writes *Tinder & Flint* books. (FYI two are already in the can, and number three has been started upon.) Maybe the reason he and Billy hit it off so well is that they have all kinds of ideas they want to get out in the world. Caffeine helps.

1) Writing the fantasy adventure series *Tinder & Flint* is totally different from your day job(s). What made you decide to put pen to paper, or more accurately, fingertips to keyboard?

I love a good story. Fantasy is great, because when I get caught up in a new world with new rules, bizarre customs and miraculous happenings, my imagination takes off. I love writing, too. In my professional life I've written lots of academic papers and non-fiction books, and I am very engaged in marketing and advocacy as a writer and speaker. I played role-playing games as a kid and stumbled back into that world by chance quite recently. I got totally absorbed in the creative process and decided to try combining some of these passions.

2) What was your writing process like?

Most of the time I close my eyes and think about the scene I'm writing. I try to see it and smell it and hear and feel it. I try to put myself in the place of the character I'm writing. Once in a while I step back and plan out larger arcs and outlines and chapter schemes. But the writing itself is immersive. Each time I sit down there's a small part of me that doesn't know if I'll be able to do it again. But before I know it, I look up and hours have passed.

3) Were you surprised by what came up?

I'm surprised every time I write. Especially nowadays deep into book three when many threads are weaving together and spawning new directions at the same time. I was surprised to find out that Gnome and X'andria met years before the others—when X'an was just a girl. That bit about their first meeting, and their first encounter with The Alchemist—that was added very late in the process.

4) What has been challenging about the writing process?

I do a lot of public speaking—I have for years. Early on I approached speeches like I might prepare a piece of classical music. I learned it, memorized it, and delivered as passionately and genuinely as possible. With time, however, I realized that my best moments of connection in public appearances were those unrehearsed moments—moments of extemporaneous commentary or elucidation. Nowadays, while I prepare extensively, my approach is very different, more a scaffolding than a script. From that scaffolding I am able to access my genuine belief in the moment of interaction with the individuals I'm speaking to. The result is more authentic communication. I have translated this to my approach to writing. I plan, to be sure, but I sit down with an openness knowing that there is no way I can possibly know what is happening until it actually happens. This is at once incredibly freeing and totally terrifying!

5) One common feature that runs throughout the book is eyes, especially *those eyes* of the demon statue. How are eyes important?

Eyes are the windows to the soul. It seems to me that as we grow up and age our bodies change around our eyes, which stay the same. My grandfather passed away recently and I was lucky to be with him near the end. I will be forever grateful for the long look we had when we said our final goodbye, he looking deep into my eyes and me looking deep into his. It was the last time we would ever look into each other's eyes. Yet I still see those pale blue eyes every single day.

6) How did the adventurers evolve in *Tinder & Flint*?

They're just getting started, of course! But Boudreaux seems to have found some people he doesn't hate. Gnome is starting to feel comfortable above ground. Arden has learned that not all of Mother Nature's creations are beautiful. Ohlen has deepened his understanding of the spiritual world. X'andria has discovered some things she's really, really interested in. And Ruprecht... whew! Ruprecht has seen some stuff he can't unsee, and now he will have to figure out how to handle it.

7) For your deserted island question, which five musical recordings would you like to have with you?

Glenn Gould playing Bach's Goldberg Variations (piano), Artur Rubenstein playing Chopin (piano), Pablo Casals playing Bach (cello), John Williams playing Agustin Barrios Mangoré (classical guitar), Dietrich Fischer-Dieskau singing Schubert's Die Schöne Müllerin.

8) And what does *Tinder & Flint* mean?

Tinder is, of course, the kindling or other material you use to make a fire. Flint is what makes the spark. Combine the two and you get fire. Fire can warm us at night, boil water for coffee and tea, and cook our food. Fire can also devastate a forest, destroy our homes, and burn us alive. In this story tinder and flint appear both literally and figuratively. Something is most definitely coming. That is the Flint. The world is the Tinder.

ABOUT THE AUTHOR

Matthew Hinsley loves a story you can crawl right into, one that grabs hold and won't let go until the ride is over. He likes heroes you can root for, who do things you might do. He doesn't like villains at all...

He and his wife Glenda live in Austin, Texas.

ABOUT THE ARTIST

Billy Garretsen is an established video game designer and artist with over 100 game credits for mobile, console and PC. He currently works with game industry veterans Gordon Walton (Ultima Online, Star Wars Galaxies) and Todd Coleman (Shadowbane, Wizard 101) at ArtCraft Entertainment where he contributes to brand development of Kickstarter success, CROWFALL™. See more of Garretsen's work on ArtStation.

CPSIA information can be obtained
at www.ICGtesting.com
Printed in the USA
LVOW08s1459170317
527609LV00001B/275/P